Please return/renew this item by the last date shown on this label, or on your self-service receipt.

To renew this item, visit **www.librarieswest.org.uk** or contact your library

Your borrower number and PIN are required.

Libraries**West**

a wish!

Here's the moment that the
little kitten, Star, gets into
Lucy's bedroom . . .

'Hey! Who are you?' Lucy laughed.

Sita came out of the bathroom wearing
her jeans and pulling a Christmassy
jumper on over her head.

'Sita of course,' she said, puzzled, and

then saw the kitten.

'Oh! It is so cute!' she said.

The tiny kitten rolled over on its back to be tickled by the girls, but then twisted around and pounced on Scruffy and Mistletoe as if expecting them to play. Then it ran to the side of the bed and jumped down.

'That's a huge leap for a little kitten!' said Lucy. 'Oh no you don't!' and she grabbed it as it started to climb up the curtains. 'This is our holiday house—we don't want you to ruin it. We'd better take you downstairs and find out who you belong to.'

To Iris - I hope you enjoy this new
Lucy Christmas story xx

OXFORD
UNIVERSITY PRESS

Great Clarendon Street, Oxford OX2 6DP
Oxford University Press is a department of the University of Oxford.
It furthers the University's objective of excellence in research, scholarship,
and education by publishing worldwide. Oxford is a registered trade mark of
Oxford University Press in the UK and in certain other countries

ISBN: 978-0-19-276663-2

1 3 5 7 9 10 8 6 4 2

Printed in Great Britain
Paper used in the production of this book is a natural,
recyclable product made from wood grown in sustainable forests.
The manufacturing process conforms to the environmental
regulations of the country of origin.

LUCY'S SEARCH
FOR LITTLE STAR

Written by Anne Booth

Illustrated by Sophy Williams

OXFORD
UNIVERSITY PRESS

Chapter One

The car headlights lit up the stone cottage at the end of the lane. The wooden door had a Christmas wreath hanging on it, and fairy lights in the windows were flashing on and off.

'Welcome to our Christmas cottage!' said Mum, stopping the car, and turning round to smile at Lucy, Gran, and Lucy's big brother, Oscar.

'Someone's been busy decorating already!' laughed Dad.

Lucy felt fizzy with excitement. After a long drive she was going to see her friend Sita again. Sita had gone back to live in Australia with her family at the beginning of the year, but she and her mum and dad had come back to England for Christmas to visit Sita's grandad, and they had rented a big holiday cottage next to a farm by the sea and had invited Lucy and her family to join them.

The front door opened and out of the brightness rushed Sita and her parents. There was lots of laughter and excitement as everyone got out of the car.

'Hello!' said Sita, a little shyly. She and Lucy had sent each other cards, and emailed and talked on Skype since she had moved back to Australia, but it felt different really being back together again.

'Hello Sita! How wonderful to see you!' said Gran, giving her a big hug, and putting her arm out to Lucy to pull her in, too. Gran made them all jump up and down, the girls laughed together, and suddenly it felt as though they had never been apart.

'I'm so glad you could all come,' said Prajit, as he carried some of their luggage and led them into the warm house.

Soon they were sitting round a big kitchen table, holding mugs of hot chocolate.

'We asked the farmer if we could decorate the house as we are staying here over Christmas, and he said "yes",' said Sita. 'We thought we could make some decorations tomorrow and buy a little Christmas tree in the town, if you like?'

'That sounds good,' said Lucy.

'You were so kind to us the first Christmas we arrived,' said Prajit. 'We wanted to treat you all.'

Sita and Lucy smiled at each other, remembering the little rabbit they had rescued and returned to his family that Christmas.

'It certainly is a treat not to have to do all the cooking for Christmas,' said Mum, 'but we can't let you do it all on your own!'

'Oscar has made a Christmas cake for us all,' said Dad.

'Good on ya, Oscar!' said Prajit.

'And Lucy and I made a Christmas pudding,' said Gran. 'We made a few, actually, to raise money for the Wildlife Rescue Centre.'

'Who will be looking after the Centre

when you are here?' Joanna asked.

'Well, that's the amazing thing,' said Gran. 'It was perfect timing! My friend Miriam, who is a retired vet, needed a holiday. She is going to stay over at my house and look after the animals, and her daughter and grandchildren are going to stay at Lucy and Oscar's and look after Merry!'

'Sorry you had to leave Merry,' said Sita to Lucy, quietly. She knew how much Lucy loved her little cat.

'It's all right,' said Lucy. 'I will miss her but I know Merry doesn't like to go away—she prefers to stay at home. And I know Miriam will make a big fuss of her.'

'I miss Twinkle too, but I know my uncle will make a big fuss of her as well,' said Sita. 'He took a picture of her yesterday and sent it to me—look.' She took out her phone and showed Lucy a sweet picture of a little black and white dog digging on a golden beach.

'When Oscar was little he tried to dig down to Australia,' said Dad. 'He thought if it was on the other side of the world he would pop up on an Australian beach.'

'Dad!' said Oscar, bringing in the cake tin from the car. 'You are so embarrassing!'

Sita's mum looked over her shoulder at the photo on the phone. 'They are going to have a barbecue on the beach for Christmas but we had to buy scarves and hats and gloves to come here!'

'Well, we won't have a barbecue, but we can definitely walk by the sea,' said Prajit.

'There is a nature reserve here too, so all you animal and bird lovers will be happy! There are even some bird hides on the dunes we can visit.'

'And look what else is here,' said Gran, pointing over at the window. 'A telescope!'

'If the skies are clear we can look at the stars,' Oscar said.

Oscar's school had a Star Centre with

a big telescope and Oscar and his friends loved it. Lucy had overheard Mum and Dad worrying that Oscar wouldn't have any friends with him over Christmas, but at least he could look at the stars. Lucy was glad she had Sita—it was so lovely to see her again.

They went upstairs to find their rooms. Sita and Lucy were sharing one at the top of the house. It was beautiful— it even had its own bathroom and a big window with a window seat. There were twin beds, each with soft white fluffy towels on them, folded and left for them to use. It was dark outside—Lucy and Sita looked at their reflections in the window and laughed and waved.

'In the morning we'll be able to see the sea from our room,' said Sita excitedly. 'You've brought Scruffy and Mistletoe!' she laughed, as she watched Lucy unpack her bag.

Lucy put Scruffy, her dog pyjama

case, and Mistletoe, her toy donkey, on the bed and finished unpacking by placing her special snow globe light on her bedside table. There was a special magic about it at this time of year, and in the past it had helped Lucy's Christmas wishes come true. She couldn't tell when it would start to glow and do its magic though, or even if there was any magic left. Most of the time it stayed a pretty snow globe, with a little cottage in a wood. It snowed when Lucy shook it, and

it had a soft light in the night which Lucy loved.

'I wonder if you will grant me a special Christmas wish again this year?' thought Lucy. She touched the cool glass globe and remembered all the magic of past Christmases. The snow globe stayed the same, but Lucy still felt hopeful. The holiday had only just begun, after all.

'I love it that you brought your snow globe!' laughed Sita, and picked it up to shake it. 'I love seeing the snow fall. I wish it would snow this Christmas!'

Lucy was sure that she saw the snow globe glow brightly for a minute as the snow fell faster and faster, although Sita didn't seem to notice. Lucy felt a little bubble of excitement rise inside.

Lucy and Sita brushed their teeth and got into bed. They had so much to talk about! Lucy told Sita all about how busy their friend Rosie's farm and café was, and how Pixie the donkey and Elf, her foal, were doing. Sita showed Lucy pictures of her friends in Australia and some of the wildlife she had seen since moving.

'I love it there, but I do miss you and Rosie. And I'm looking forward to seeing Grandad tomorrow,' said Sita. 'He is bringing Charlie, his spaniel, with him! And Oscar will love talking to my grandad because he knows so much about the stars.'

Sita gave a big yawn and snuggled down under the covers.

Lucy leant over and shook the globe so that the snow fell over the little house in the woods inside. 'Please let it snow

for Sita this Christmas,' she whispered quietly. The globe lit up brightly for a second and Lucy felt a tingling excitement run through her. Was it her imagination or could she hear tinkling sleigh bells? Lucy felt a little Christmassy flutter of happiness.

'Goodnight Lucy—I can't wait to explore tomorrow morning! I think this Christmas is going to be so much fun!' said Sita.

'I do too,' said Lucy, and glanced over at the snow globe. 'And maybe a little magical too,' she said hopefully to herself, as she drifted off to sleep.

Chapter Two

Lucy and Sita slept in late the next day.
Lucy felt Mistletoe's soft ears next to her
on the pillow, and opened her eyes. She
wasn't quite sure where she was at first,
but it was great to see Sita sitting up in

the next bed to hers. They were on holiday!

'Morning!' said Sita. 'Mum's gone to get Grandad already and Oscar has gone with your dad and mine to get a Christmas tree.'

Sita jumped out of bed and pulled back the curtains. Outside Lucy could see a little garden, with a bird table and a pond. Behind that were fields with sheep, and behind that, sand dunes and the sea, glinting in the winter sunshine. The sky was a clear blue.

'Let's get washed and dressed quickly and then go and explore after breakfast,' said Sita.

Lucy had a quick shower, got dressed

and made the bed. Scruffy the pyjama-case dog had fallen on the floor next to Sita's bed.

'Where do you think you are going?' said Lucy, putting him back next to Mistletoe on the pillow. She wondered how her cat Merry was doing back at home, and just at that moment she heard a little miaow outside the bedroom door.

Lucy shook her head: she must have imagined it. But then she heard it again! She opened the door, and felt something soft against her leg: she looked down and saw an adorable tiny ginger kitten which ran right past her, jumped up on the bed, and settled down next to Mistletoe and Scruffy.

'Hey! Who are you?' Lucy laughed.

Sita came out of the bathroom wearing
her jeans and pulling a Christmassy
jumper on over her head.

'Sita of course,' she said, puzzled,
and then saw the kitten.

'Oh! It is so cute!' she said.

The tiny kitten rolled over on its
back to be tickled by the girls, but then

twisted around and pounced on Scruffy and Mistletoe as if expecting them to play. Then it ran to the side of the bed and jumped down.

'That's a huge leap for a little kitten!' said Lucy. 'Oh no you don't!' and she grabbed it as it started to climb up the curtains. 'This is our holiday house—we don't want you to ruin it. We'd better take you downstairs and find out who you belong to.'

It was nice holding a fluffy warm kitten. It was bright and inquisitive with beautiful big blue eyes.

'What a sweet kitten!' said Lucy's mum as they came into the kitchen.

'Trust you to find an animal, Lucy!'

'But where on earth did it come from?' said Gran. 'It must have run inside and up the stairs when the others opened the door to go out. I wonder if it belongs to the farmer next door? There are no other houses nearby.'

'I'll take it round,' said Lucy, and she and Sita went a little further down the lane to the farmer's house. It didn't look very Christmassy compared to the holiday cottage, and when Lucy knocked at the door, the old man who opened it looked a bit grumpy. The kitten jumped down out of Lucy's arms and rubbed itself against his legs and disappeared into the house.

'We brought your kitten back,' Lucy said, smiling.

'Why, where was he?' The farmer didn't smile back.

Lucy was a bit surprised. 'He came up into our bedroom.'

'Well, I can't do anything about that. He wanders off. If you leave your door open he will be inside. There's nothing I can do about it.'

'Oh—we didn't mind,' said Lucy. 'We love kittens. He is so sweet. What is his name?'

'No need to be calling him any names,' said the farmer. 'He's here

to catch mice in the farm, not to be petted by holidaymakers,' and he closed the door on them.

The girls looked at each other.

'Well, that wasn't very nice!' said Sita. 'He didn't even say thank you.'

'I know!' said Lucy. 'Poor kitten, living with him,' and they went back to the holiday cottage.

'Maybe his bark is worse than his bite,' said Gran, ladling out some porridge for the girls.

'Don't let it spoil your morning,' said Mum.

'If the kitten comes back I'm going to make a real fuss of him,' said Lucy. 'What a mean old man.'

They added honey and raisins to the porridge. It was hot and creamy and eating it made them feel much better.

Then they heard a car draw up outside and an excited bark.

The door opened and Sita's mum came in with a very smiley grey-haired man with a little beard and glasses. He gave Sita an enormous hug.

'Grandad!' she said, beaming.

A little brown and white spaniel
rushed in and all about, wagging his tail
and barking happily.

'Shh, Charlie,' said Sita's grandad. Charlie sat, and tried not to make a noise, but he looked as if it was very hard for him not to jump about, and a funny little whine came out. Lucy loved him.

'Can I stroke him?' she asked.

'Of course!' said Sita's grandad. 'I'm trying to get him not to jump up, but he keeps forgetting. Stop stroking him when he jumps and he will get the message.'

Charlie was so soft and loving. He butted his head against Lucy almost as if he was a cat, and when he got over-excited and started putting his paws up on her legs she stopped stroking him and he sat down again.

'He's a real lapdog,' said Joanna.
'That dog loves cuddles.'

Lucy went over to the rocking chair
and Charlie pattered over and sat in front
of her, his mouth open so it looked like
he was smiling.

'I think he wants to be picked up,'
said Gran.

Lucy bent down and scooped him up in her arms and he gave her a big lick on the nose. Then he cuddled down on her lap, all soft and warm and furry, and put his head on her arm.

Soon Oscar, Dad, and Prajit were back too. They bustled into the kitchen carrying a Christmas tree, and Charlie went mad all over again, jumping off Lucy's lap and barking.

'Hey, little fella, it's just a tree,' said Prajit.

Oscar and Dad put the tree in the corner of the large kitchen and Oscar turned and squatted down to talk to Charlie. He fondled the spaniel's soft brown ears and spoke to him quietly, and Charlie's tail started wagging again.

'Let's decorate the tree, shall we?' said Sita's grandad.

He brought out newspaper which he spread on the kitchen table, then lots of pine cones, scissors, paper, some glue and glitter and felt and paints and stick-on eyes.

'This is fun!' said Lucy's gran, sitting at the table.

'You're very organized!' said Lucy's mum.

'Dad used to be an art teacher, so he has always been good at things like this,' said Joanna, smiling over at him.

'It's nice to have a reason for doing

it,' he said. 'Now, Oscar, I hear you are interested in stars?'

Oscar went red and looked a bit shy but pleased.

'I wonder . . . if you're not into pine cone animals, would you like to have a go at origami?' he asked. 'We need a star for the top of the tree and I've brought the instructions and some special paper, if you're up for it?'

Oscar nodded, still stroking Charlie.

'I brought paper chains for us to make as well,' said Gran, 'and some tinsel to hang on the tree too.'

'Great minds think alike!' said Sita's grandad.

31

'And I'll play this Christmas music on my phone whilst you do it,' said Dad, putting on some Christmas songs. 'Prajit and I will get on and make some lunch.'

'Talk about football, you mean!' said Mum.

'That as well,' said Dad, grabbing her and quickly waltzing round the table. He gave her a kiss on the cheek before going over to the cooker at the far end of the room.

Lucy looked across the table at Mum, laughing with Joanna as they made funny pine cone animals, and Oscar, frowning with concentration as he read the instructions for the origami star and started folding the paper.

'I'm making a pine cone donkey!' said Lucy. 'Look!'

'I'm making an owl,' said Sita, reaching out for the brown felt so she could cut out wings.

'After lunch, let's all go for a walk to the sea through the nature reserve,' said Sita's grandad.

'That sounds great,' said Gran. 'Doesn't it Lucy?'

'Yes,' said Lucy, smiling back and feeling Charlie's soft head as he woke up and sleepily rested it on her foot under the table. Apart from the grumpy farmer, this holiday was already lots of fun and she had a feeling it was going to get even better.

Chapter Three

The funny pine cone animals were hung on the tree, and Oscar had finished his origami star and placed it in pride of place at the very top.

When Lucy was outside, putting

the paper in the recycling bin, the little ginger kitten came up to her for a fuss.

'I wish you had a name,' said Lucy as she bent down to stroke him. Just then she noticed a little patch of white fur on his back. 'It looks like a star,' she said. 'I don't care what that grumpy farmer says, I am going to

call you Star. Would you like that?' The kitten wound himself in and out of her legs, purring even louder.

'Sorry I have to go now, little Star,' said Lucy. 'But I'll see you later, I promise.'

Mum had placed a Christmas tablecloth on the kitchen table and lit a candle, so that when Dad brought in a delicious pasta dish it felt like a special holiday meal. Prajit had made chocolate brownies for pudding.

'These are delicious!' said Gran. 'I had no idea you were such a good cook.'

'Let's have a Christmas bake off,' said Dad.

'You're on!' said Prajit.

'If everyone decides on what they are going to make today, then I will get the ingredients,' said Mum. 'We can't all use the oven at the same time, and we don't want to make too many things.'

'I liked it when we decorated biscuits,' said Sita.

'Let's each make biscuits then,' said Mum. 'And decorate them too!'

After all the things had been cleared away Dad went out to the car to bring in the family's wellies. He left the door ajar, and they had an unexpected visitor.

Charlie was being fussed by Sita and Lucy, and nobody noticed Star until the tiny kitten had come in and gone right up behind Charlie. He got very interested in Charlie's tail, which was wagging on the floor, and pounced on it, which made Charlie jump up and bark, and the kitten ran off.

'Hey, Star, don't be naughty!' said Lucy, picking the kitten up. Star wriggled out of her arms and ran back to Charlie.

'He isn't frightened at all!' said Sita.

Charlie was being very good. He backed off from the kitten, but his tail was wagging really fast, as though he wanted to play.

Just then the kitten noticed Oscar's laces were undone and pounced on them, before running out of the door again. Everyone laughed and Charlie gave a little woof.

'What a funny little thing,' Lucy smiled.

***

It was fun walking to the sea. The air smelt different, and Lucy liked hearing the gulls calling in the sky.

'We're lucky to have this nature reserve,' said Sita's grandad. 'We have the sea and the dunes, but we also have little lakes, or loughs, too, and the farmers' fields.'

'What are those dark-coloured ducks called?' said Lucy, pointing to some birds pecking the grass in a field.

'Those are Brent geese,' said Sita's grandad. 'They are overwintering with us here.'

'Where have they come from?' said Lucy.

'They may have come from Canada, or from Svalbard, which is up above Norway, towards the North Pole,' said Sita's grandad.

'I wonder if they know Santa!' laughed Dad, and ruffled Lucy's hair.

'Dad!' said Lucy.

Charlie was very interested in the

rabbit warrens in the sand dunes, but they didn't let him off the lead until they got down to the beach. Oscar threw some sticks for him, and the rest of the time Charlie stuck his nose into rock pools and ran around sniffing everywhere. Then he ran to the frothy edge of the waves but he didn't like the way they came towards him.

43

'They are playing with him just like Star did,' laughed Lucy.

'Do you think there's a chance of a white Christmas by the sea?' Sita asked.

'Snow doesn't often settle here, so I doubt it,' said Sita's grandad.

'I'd love it to snow so much,' said Sita.

'If my Christmas wish comes true, it will!' Lucy thought to herself.

'It's certainly cold enough for snow,' said Joanna. 'Brr, I think it's time to go back in the warm.'

Just then there was a loud sound of honking, almost like car horns, and they all looked up. A group of beautiful, snow white swans flew overhead, the sounds of their wings making a soft hissing noise as they passed above them.

'Oh, lovely!' said Gran, a big smile on her face. 'Whooper swans. Their wings make a particular sound when they pass over. I love them. They migrate as families from Iceland—the parents look after the cygnets in the summer when they hatch, and then they all fly here in the winter together.'

'Like us,' said Prajit, hugging Sita.

'Then they fly back together in the spring,' said Gran.

'Not like us,' said Sita, a little sadly. 'We go in the New Year.'

'They do come back to the same place every year,' said Sita's grandad.

'That's a good idea!' said Prajit.

'Let's enjoy the holiday whilst we are here and go back to the cottage,' said Joanna. 'I think it's time for some hot drinks and maybe a Christmas film.'

'I wish Star had a proper family too,' thought Lucy. 'Maybe I could make a second wish on the snow globe for Star to have an owner who really loves him?'

Back at the cottage, Star was waiting for them on the doorstep.

Chapter Four

Lucy grinned and scooped Star up in her arms, taking him inside and sitting down on the sofa with him.

He looked up at her and purred, then curled up and went to sleep as Lucy and Sita watched a very funny Christmas cartoon together. Charlie lay under Sita's grandad's chair and went to sleep. He didn't want a kitten pouncing on him.

Then Star decided he wanted to go outside and miaowed at the door until they let him out. He disappeared into the dark.

'It's so cold outside,' Lucy worried.

'He'll probably go straight home,' said Gran.

'I hope the farmer lets him in,' Lucy said. While everyone was busy downstairs, Lucy rushed up to her room and held her snow globe tightly. 'I know I wished for a white Christmas but I have one more, small wish for you. Please grant Star a happy home with someone who really loves him.' Lucy shook the globe and watched the snow fall. It seemed like the pretty little snow globe was glowing a little brighter, but there was nothing like the whirling, glittering snow that Lucy normally saw when it was granting a wish. Lucy sighed, but she knew that you couldn't make the snow globe do anything if it didn't want to.

Back downstairs, Oscar was looking through the telescope at the bright night sky.

'It's a cold night and there is no cloud, so the sky is very clear,' said Oscar, excitedly.

Oscar showed the others three bright
stars in a row. 'You can see them even
without the telescope. They're called
Orion's belt,' Oscar said.

'I think we say those three stars are

the handle of a saucepan,' said Prajit.

'Who was Orion?' said Sita.

'Legend says he was a hunter, and the stars under his belt are a sword hanging down,' said Sita's grandad.

'If you look down left from those three stars you can see a very bright star—that's called Sirius, the dog star,' said Oscar.

'Did you hear that, Charlie?' said Gran. Charlie was asleep, but he opened one eye and slowly wagged his tail when he heard his name.

'If you go back to the belt and look through this telescope down at the stars under it, the ones they call the sword, you can see a glowing mist around one of them,' said Oscar. 'It's almost like two bird wings, one on either side, and in the centre of the glow there are actually lots of stars being made, a sort of star nursery.'

'I can see the mist!' said Sita, excitedly, looking through the telescope. 'It's amazing to think of baby stars!'

Lucy thought of baby Star, the little kitten. She hoped he wasn't still outside.

'Can I check on the kitten, Gran?' she said.

'I'm sure he is inside in the warm,' said Gran, 'but I'll come with you and look.'

They went outside. The sky was very

beautiful. It was easy to see the three stars of Orion the hunter's belt, but there was no sign of the kitten.

'I am sure he is curled up cosily at home,' said Gran.

The next morning Lucy woke up early and couldn't get back to sleep. She couldn't stop thinking about little Star.

Lucy leant across and took the snow globe in her hands. She felt its cool roundness, shook it so that the snow fell on the cottage, and closed her eyes.

'Please Snow Globe—don't forget little Star. He needs you.'

Even though Lucy should have felt

disappointed that her wishes hadn't come true yet, she didn't. Her snow globe had never let her down before. She just had to wait for the magic.

Lucy was now wide awake, so she got dressed quietly and went downstairs. Gran and Sita's grandad were already up and chatting.

'Hello Lucy,' said Gran. 'We're just having an early morning cup of tea and a natter over toast and jam. Would you like some? Then we are going to walk Charlie—do you want to come?'

It was fun going for a walk in the early morning. On the beach there were black and white wading birds with red legs and beaks—oystercatchers—carefully walking over the wet sand and putting their long red beaks into it, investigating for food. They flew away with peeping whistling calls when Charlie ran up to them, but Lucy saw them land a little further down the beach to continue their search.

After a bracing walk on the beach they headed home, and as they got nearer to the cottage Lucy saw a tiny ginger figure on the path, and smiled as the little kitten ran up to her. Charlie wagged his tail as Star sniffed him, but Star was more interested in rubbing against Lucy. She picked him up and he nuzzled into Lucy's neck.

'Good morning!' said Gran, as the farmer overtook them on the path.

'Morning,' said the farmer, but didn't smile, as he looked over at Lucy, cuddling Star.

'Do you think it might snow?' said

Gran.

'Could do. Sky looks grey enough,' said the farmer. 'Cold enough, too, for a white Christmas. Come on you then— breakfast,' and he walked on ahead, as little Star jumped out of Lucy's arms and followed the farmer.

'Poor little Star,' Lucy muttered. 'He needs cuddles and love as well as breakfast.'

Chapter Five

'Why do you call the kitten Star?' Gran asked Lucy.

'Because he has a white star shape on his back,' said Lucy. 'And because it isn't right the farmer doesn't call him by a name.'

'We don't call all the wild animals we rescue by names, though, do we, Lucy?'

'But that's different. We don't want to get too fond of them or make them pets. That farmer *should* get fond of Star,' said Lucy.

She felt a bit cross with Gran, sticking up for that grumpy man.

She stomped upstairs to find the snow globe. She could hear Sita in the shower, so she knew she had a few minutes. She took it in her hands again.

'Hello Snow Globe,' she said. 'It's me again. You HAVE to help little Star. That farmer is awful. I can look after Star whilst we are here, but my Christmas wish

is for Little Star to have a forever home
with someone to love him.'

Suddenly the globe lit up brightly
in Lucy's hands and she felt a tingling
excitement run up into her arms, up

to her head and down to her toes. The sound of tinkling sleigh bells was unmistakable. Lucy was glad the water in the shower was still running so Sita wouldn't hear. Inside the globe the snow fell faster and faster, this time in all colours of the rainbow, round and round whilst the bells kept tinkling. The globe was warm in her hands and Lucy had a feeling that everything was going to be absolutely fine.

Then it stopped, and the snow globe was cool again and looked quite normal as Sita came out of the shower.

'You look happy,' said Sita.

'I am!' beamed Lucy. 'I think this is

going to be a great holiday.'

Back in the warm, Charlie was glad to go and curl up in his basket in the kitchen, and everyone else went out to the town to do Christmas shopping at the market. The Christmas lights looked lovely, there was a brass band playing Christmas carols, and the smell of roast chestnuts in the air. Sita and Lucy had such a nice time together and Lucy kept feeling happy about the snow globe.

They got some sparkly green and gold wrapping paper on one stall and a cat toy to bring home for her cat Merry, and a feather toy for Star on another.

'I bet that farmer won't get him anything,' Lucy thought.

Sita went off to buy a secret present for Lucy, and Lucy bought some Christmas socks with kittens on which were perfect for Sita, some gloves for Mum, and a book about origami for Oscar.

'I can't believe I've finished my Christmas shopping!' she said to everyone when they all met up at the car park as arranged. Everyone was cheerful, carrying lots of mysterious bags and packages. Gran said her shopping had gone very well too. Oscar had a bag and looked very pleased. Everyone looked full of happy secrets.

Charlie was very pleased to see them when they got home, and delighted when Oscar said he would take him for a walk. Sita and Lucy went upstairs and wrapped up Christmas presents whilst Mum made a lovely stew and they had it for lunch with fresh crusty bread from the market

when Oscar and a rather wet and sandy
Charlie got back.

Lucy looked out of the window.

'Oh no! There's a tractor parked in
the farmyard and little Star has climbed
right up to the top of it. He is on the roof.
I'm sure that's dangerous. He is too tiny

to be up there. I bet there are all sorts of rusty things on the ground if he fell off. I'm going to get him.'

Sita and Lucy rushed out and stood by the tractor. Little Star looked down, his big eyes wide.

'How did he get up there?' said Sita, and as if to show her, little Star ran over to a branch of a tree next to the tractor's roof, jumped on to it and down the tree and ran over to the girls, purring loudly and rubbing himself against their legs.

'You've had a big adventure, haven't you Star,' Lucy said as she came back into the house holding the tiny kitten. 'You were a bit silly, weren't you?' she said to the little purring cat.

'Are you sure it's a good idea to bring him into the house again Lucy?' said Gran. 'You don't want him to get too fond of us. Merry is your cat, not this kitten, and he is a farm cat, after all. He has to get used to a farmyard.' But Lucy pretended she hadn't heard.

Star was such fun. He played so much he got tired out and fell asleep on Lucy's bed curled up with Mistletoe and Scruffy.

Sita and Lucy listened to some music and chatted, and then Star woke up and scratched to be let out. Lucy opened the door and he ran down the stairs and miaowed until Dad let him out the front door.

'I'll really miss him when we go,' said Lucy.

'I know—he is so sweet,' said Sita.

Lucy didn't want to talk to Gran on her own that evening. 'I think my wish on the snow globe has given me an idea,' she said to herself. She was thinking of asking for a very special present from her mum and dad. Somehow, however, she didn't want Gran to know about it.

'What's happening about the baking competition?' Lucy asked Mum.

'Good point Lucy!' said Mum. 'Right everyone—time to plan your biscuits. There are some books in the cottage if you need to look up recipes, or you can use Dad's laptop. Then, when you have chosen your ingredients, write them down and give your list to me and I will go out and buy them tomorrow.'

Everyone got very competitive, and it was easy for Lucy to avoid talking to Gran. She pretended to be so busy looking for a special biscuit recipe that she didn't have time.

Then they had dinner, and she and Sita watched a film and cuddled Charlie, and then, whilst Gran was busy playing cards with Oscar, Lucy and Sita went to bed.

Sita fell asleep straight away, but Lucy lay and shook the snow globe.

'I know you are going to make sure Star has a happy home now,' she said. 'I think that's why you have given me this idea. I am going to ask Mum and Dad if they will buy Star the kitten from the farmer,' said Lucy, as she watched the snow fall. 'Merry will like to have a friend, and it is much better for a kitten to have someone to love him. I love him so much and I will keep him safe.'

The snow fell as normal in the shaken globe, but somehow watching it fall on the pretty cottage in the woods didn't make Lucy feel as Christmassy as it normally did. Lucy usually gave Gran a kiss goodnight when she was staying with them but tonight she had rushed upstairs without saying anything. Lucy felt a bit bad remembering it.

'I'll talk to her tomorrow after Mum and Dad have agreed about Star,' decided Lucy. The snow had stopped falling and inside the globe it was just a wintry scene of a cottage in a wood. The light wasn't very bright either.

'I'll ask Mum if we can buy a new battery,' thought Lucy, as she drifted off to sleep. 'It isn't working as well as it normally does.'

The next morning Lucy stayed in bed reading until Gran and the others had left to go shopping.

Lucy got out of bed, being careful not to wake Sita, and tiptoed downstairs. She put her boots and warm coat and hat and gloves on, and went out to look for Star.

Outside the air was very cold and Lucy's breath made little clouds in the air.

'I hope Star comes over to our house to keep warm,' she said to herself. Even though it was morning the clouds in the sky made it still quite dark. The sky looked heavy and light grey, and nearer than normal.

'I wonder if it is going to snow?' said Lucy. 'Sita would love that.'

Lucy walked a little way down the lane. A robin on a hedge perched and sang at her, his red breast bright in the dark day.

Suddenly she heard a little 'miaow' and she looked down to see Star had suddenly appeared, purring at her feet.

Lucy picked him up. His fur was cold and he climbed up Lucy so he could touch noses with her, his little body vibrating with purrs.

'I'll take you home and you can meet

Merry,' whispered Lucy.

He gave a little wriggle and jumped down, running down the lane back to the cottages.

Lucy's tummy gave a rumble and she suddenly shivered with the cold. She meant what she had said to Star—she did want to bring him home to live with Merry, but now she was feeling nervous about what she was going to ask Mum and Dad. 'I hope they know how horrible the farmer is,' she worried. 'And what if they have got me a present already? I could ask them to take it back. I don't care what I get for Christmas really,' she said to herself as she walked back to the cottage. The fairy lights were flashing and it looked warm and welcoming. She suddenly couldn't wait to get back inside.

Charlie seemed to know Lucy was coming back and woofed at the door as Lucy got to it. Sita's grandad opened it, smiling.

'Just in time for my special pancakes, Lucy,' he said. 'Come into the warm— you look frozen!'

Sita was up and Lucy joined her for a wonderful pancake breakfast. Then the others were back from the shops,

unloading lots of special food and drinks and treats for Christmas.

'We're going to have a feast!' said Mum.

'Let's go for a good walk before lunch,' said Gran. 'I think it might snow today, so we should go sooner rather than later.'

Everyone put on their warmest clothes, Sita put Charlie on his lead, and they set out. The little ginger kitten was waiting outside, and started to follow Lucy.

'Oh goodness, we don't want the kitten following us,' said Gran, and gently shooed it away. 'Go on, go home. This is too long a walk for you. We don't want you getting lost.'

The kitten ran off a little way and then stopped and watched them.

'What if it snows whilst we are on the walk?' worried Lucy. 'I bet the farmer won't think to bring him inside. I wish we could take him with us,' she thought. 'I could wrap him up and carry him inside my coat. He'd look so sweet.'

They walked a little bit further along the lane. Charlie was pulling Sita along as she talked to her grandad. Oscar and Prajit were arguing happily about football, and Gran and Mum and Dad and Joanna were talking together at the front. Lucy glanced back and noticed a tiny ginger shape running up the road after them. She smiled.

'I won't call him, because Gran will get cross, but I'm sure Star will catch up with us soon. I can always carry him home in my pocket if he gets tired,' Lucy thought with a shiver of happiness.

Chapter Six

There was so much to see on the walk. Sita's grandad pointed out a short-eared owl sitting on a stone wall, gazing calmly at them in the low daylight, until it flew away. It was so cold, the clouds seemed darker and heavier all the time, and there was a still, expectant feeling in the air.

'If we have a white Christmas my wish will have come true,' Sita squealed.

Lucy noticed little Star was keeping his distance but still trotting behind them. She was quite pleased, because the further he followed them, the harder it would be to send him back. 'He won't have to be out in any cold snow,' thought Lucy. 'He can sit on my knee in the pub later. He'll probably go to sleep!'

Down at the beach, the cold air was full of the sounds of gulls of all sorts, calling and beating the air with their wings. The sea whooshed and rattled the shingle as the waves went back and forth over them.

Lucy looked for Star but she couldn't see the little ginger kitten anywhere.

'Is everything OK, Lucy?' said Gran.

'Yes,' said Lucy. She knew that wasn't true. 'Well, actually I was worrying about Star the kitten. I can't see him anywhere. He started following us again after you sent him back.'

'Oh, don't worry. He won't have followed us far. He will have soon got bored and gone home. He'll be all curled up by a warm fire by now,' said Gran.

Lucy didn't feel all that sure. Gran thought Star had turned back near to the cottage. What would she think if she knew he had gone much further? And what would she think of Lucy if she knew Lucy had seen him following them and had not done anything?

'A warm fire? That's a good idea! Time for our pub lunch I think!' said Dad. 'Come on Lucy, let's have a race along the beach!'

Even though the pies were delicious, Lucy kept worrying about Star. Where had she seen him last? Was it after they had seen the owl? Did he go on the beach?

When they walked back Lucy looked all over the beach to see if she could spot him, checking near the rock pools too.

'Have you lost something?' said Mum.

'I'm just worried about Star, the kitten,' said Lucy. 'I'm worried he followed us.' She was beginning to feel awful that she hadn't said anything about it when she had noticed him following them. She had been so sure she would be able to pick him up and look after him. She hadn't expected him to run off.

'He wouldn't have come this far,' said Mum. 'Don't worry, Lucy. He'll be asleep on the farmer's lap right now, I'm sure.

'Look!' said Sita. 'Is that snow falling?'

'Yes!' said Prajit. 'You've got your

wish, Sita. Looks like it will be a white Christmas after all.'

They scrambled back up from the beach and hurried along the lanes back to the cottage. The red-breasted robin sang at them from a hedge, as all around it got whiter and whiter as the snow fell faster and faster.

'It's like a Christmas card!' said Sita happily.

When they got back to the cottage Lucy looked around outside for little Star, but she couldn't see him anywhere. The farmer's cottage had its lights on and the curtains were drawn. He had left them more logs for the fire, dry and protected from the snow in a bag on the doorstep.

'That's kind of him,' said Gran. She made up the fire quickly whilst Mum found some marshmallows and put them on sticks so that they could toast them. Joanna made them all hot chocolate and they sat round, laughing and telling jokes, watching the flames dancing around the wood and listening to the cheery crackle.

Lucy looked out of the window anxiously. It was like when she shook her snow globe—all she could see was snow falling outside. It was getting darker now.

Oscar came to look out of the window too.

'Do you think the kitten is out there?' said Lucy.

'No,' said Oscar. 'He won't like the snow. He is like Merry. He will be in the warm with the farmer.'

'Are you worrying about the kitten

still?' said Gran. 'You are a kind girl, Lucy. I'm sure the farmer is keeping him safe out of the snow. He looks after his animals very well.'

Later on, before bed, they had hot tomato soup and bread rolls.

'It's Christmas Eve tomorrow,' said Dad. 'Let's have our baking competition and then go to the midnight carol service

in town.'

'That sounds great!' said Joanna.

'This is the best Christmas holiday ever!' said Sita as she got ready for bed. Lucy looked out of the window at the snow, still falling heavily, the flakes lit up in the moonlight. The garden and the fields behind it glowed softly white in the night.

When Lucy saw that Sita was asleep she shook the snow globe again.

'Thank you for granting Sita's wish— but I have got an even more important wish now. I hope you still have magic left as you have just got to help me. I am so sorry I didn't pick Star up when I saw him. I wish I had.' The snow globe didn't glow or change in any way.

'Maybe I can't wish in the past,' Lucy said, feeling awful. 'I should have listened to Gran and sent him back. I just hope Gran is right and he is with the farmer. He is such a clever little kitten—I am sure he found his way back. He must have.'

Lucy eventually fell asleep. She dreamt about Star being lost in the snow, hiding from owls and gulls swooping around looking for him. The farmer was riding around on a robin, and Star was in a boat, drifting out to sea and Lucy couldn't reach him. She was glad to wake up.

'It's Christmas Eve!' said Sita, happily. 'And look! It's still snowing and the snow is really deep! We can build a snowman!'

They went downstairs to join everyone else for breakfast. Lucy was glad when Gran went to answer a knock at the door and the farmer was there.

'Morning,' he said.

'Thanks so much for the logs,' said Gran. 'We've been lovely and cosy in your cottage.'

'I was wondering if you have my kitten with you?' said the farmer. 'He didn't come home last night. I thought he might be in the barn, but he isn't there. I know that little girl likes him . . .' He looked over at Lucy.

'Oh dear,' said Gran. 'No, we haven't seen him since he tried to follow us on our walk yesterday, have we, Lucy? I made sure to shoo him away and we hadn't even passed the gate by then.'

'I saw him a bit later,' said Lucy, going red, but she knew she just had to tell the truth now. Star wasn't at home. This was awful. Where was Star?

'Yes, you said that,' said Gran. 'But he didn't follow us far, did he?'

'Well—I can't remember really. I saw him a few times,' admitted Lucy.

'Where?' said the farmer, sounding cross.

'I saw him when we passed the sheep field, and I saw him . . . I think it was near the dunes.'

'Near the dunes?' said the farmer. 'But that's a good way away. You should never have let him follow you that far. I'll have to go and find him.' With that the farmer turned on his heel and left.

'Why didn't you say he was at the dunes?' said Oscar. 'You should have said last night.'

Lucy burst into tears and Sita put her

arms around her.

'He'll be all right,' said Dad. 'Animals know how to look after themselves and find warm places.'

The rest of the day seemed to go very slowly for Lucy. She went upstairs and tried wishing and shaking the snow globe. 'I wish that the farmer finds little Star safe and sound.'

To her relief she felt the globe grow warm in her hands and the telltale tingling feeling rushed through her. Lucy waited all day for the farmer to come back with Star but there was no sign of either of them.

'I know you glowed when I made my

wish. I felt you were listening,' she said to the snow globe. 'Even if it is the last wish I ever have—I want it to be that he is OK.'

It had started snowing again, even heavier now. Lucy wrapped presents and helped Mum make lunch, and everybody made biscuits for the decorating competition that evening, but all the time she was thinking about little Star.

'Shall I go and ask the farmer if he has found the kitten yet?' said Dad after dinner, noticing how quiet Lucy was.

'Yes please,' said Lucy. Dad went and came back quite quickly. Lucy could tell from his serious face that he didn't have good news.

'Has he found him?' she asked.

'Now Lucy, I'm sure he is safe and warm somewhere, but no, not yet. I'm sure he found somewhere to shelter,' said Dad.

'But he is just a baby, and it's getting dark outside. It is all my fault,' cried Lucy, and ran upstairs. She closed the door, flung herself on her bed and gathered Scruffy and Mistletoe in her arms and cried on them. She looked over at the snow globe by her bed.

'I'm going to put this right, Snow Globe. I'm going to find little Star,' said Lucy.

Chapter Seven

Lucy put the snow globe in her pocket. 'If you have any magic left in you, I need you right now,' she said.

Lucy slipped downstairs. She could hear everyone talking in the kitchen.

'Poor Lucy,' she heard Sita say.

'Let her have a little cry by herself,' said Joanna. 'She looks worn out. I'm sure he is safe and sound in a shed somewhere. He won't like the snow.'

Lucy silently took her coat and hat and gloves, and put her wellies on, going out into the snow before anyone noticed and tried to stop her.

It was dusk, and the snow had stopped falling. The countryside looked so different under its new cold white blanket, eerie and a little strange. The snow was deep already, and crunched around Lucy's boots as she walked as fast as she could down the lane towards the dunes. Lucy didn't have time to look at how lovely it was—all she was interested in was seeing a little ginger kitten against the white, but she couldn't see him anywhere. A flock of black crows rose up into the sky, cawing. Lucy's breath came out in clouds in the cold. The sun was going down now, and already she could see tiny stars appearing.

She went as fast as she could, looking from side to side as she ran down the long lane by the fields. It was hard running in deep snow in wellingtons, and she slipped and stumbled, and felt more and more worried and upset as she went. She got to the sand dunes, now covered in snow, and ran around, and up and down, calling as she went.

'Little Star! Little Star! Don't be afraid! I'm here!' She could hear the steady sound of the sea in the background. It seemed very loud, and her own voice, calling Star, sounded very thin and quiet.

Then she looked around and realized she was completely lost on the dunes. She had no idea where she was any more. Everything looked so unfamiliar in the snow. The stars were bright but looked very far away in the clear night sky and she suddenly felt scared.

'Maybe the snow globe can help me

now,' she said, and reached for it in her pocket, but it wasn't there.

'Oh no!' said Lucy. 'I must have dropped it when I was running.' She suddenly felt very cold and alone.

'Please, Snow Globe,' she called out into the snowstorm. The wind across the dunes took her words and carried them away across the winter sea so she could hardly hear them herself. 'I can't see you—but please listen! I need your help more than ever. Little Star is lost and now I am too. Please give me this Christmas wish and help us get home.'

She shivered in the cold and dark and felt her teeth chatter. She peered desperately into the night, looking for a sign. At first nothing happened but then she heard the faint sound of sleigh bells and saw something glowing in the distance.

Her heart started thudding. She could hardly dare believe that the globe could have granted her wish. Lucy listened out and carefully trudged towards the glowing light, and as she got nearer she could see that the globe was lying on the snow, shining brighter than she had ever seen it before. She never felt so relieved about anything. She picked the globe up and it warmed her hands.

'I found you!' she said, hugging it
to her chest. 'Thank you so, so much.
Please, please help me find Star and get
us both home safe,' she said, and shook
it. As Lucy watched the snowflakes fall,
the snow inside the globe seemed to
suddenly be outside until she was totally

surrounded by white, and then red and blue and green and rainbow-coloured, sparkling, glittering snow which twisted and turned and narrowed down, changing into a long, dancing ribbon of tiny stars in the air in front of her. She put out her hand to it, and she felt it like a rope she could hold and follow. Lucy looked up at the stars, shining brightly in the now clear sky. She could see the three stars of Orion's belt and Sirius the dog star.

'Please may there be a kitten star somewhere,' she wished.

She put her hand on the glittering rope of stars and felt it warm and tingly under her gloves. It led her across the snow to a small rabbit hole, and then disappeared. There, peeping out, was a cold and wet ginger kitten with two big blue eyes. He was shivering, and his wet fur made him look even tinier than ever.

'Oh Star,' Lucy said, picking him up and cuddling him. 'I am so sorry I let you get lost.'

She put him in her coat pocket beside the warm snow globe, which was glowing brightly now, and warming them both up.

'Now, how can we get home?' Lucy said out loud, and put her hand on the globe. She found herself looking up at the stars again, at Orion's Belt and the dog star.

'I can remember that we saw them through our cottage window—so if I walk away from them now I should be heading in the right direction. Is that a good idea, Snow Globe?' Lucy asked. The globe glowed brightly and Lucy suddenly felt confident and happy and excited.

'I know you will help me if I go wrong—but I think I can do this by looking at the stars,' she said, and set off in the direction she thought would bring her off the dunes. It helped that she found her old footsteps in the snow, and sure enough, she soon found herself back on the road.

'I've done it!' she said with relief. 'I've navigated by the stars!' After feeling so bad about Star, she couldn't help feeling proud of herself. She found more of her old footsteps in the snow and quickly got back on the lane. Soon she saw the flashing lights of the holiday cottage, warm and welcoming and bright in the darkness of the night.

The curtains were drawn and the fairy lights were twinkling. Lucy felt very tired and happy. There was a sound of sleigh bells and the snow globe glowed brightly again. She was standing outside in the dark, in the snow, little Star safe and sound and drying out, cuddled up next to the warm globe in her pocket, and the cottage door was opening.

Chapter Eight

'Lucy!' said Gran, who was dressed in her coat and hat. 'We were just coming out to look for you. We have only just realized you weren't here. Where on earth have you been?' Gran brought Lucy inside.

'Oh Lucy!' said Dad 'We were so worried! Thank goodness you are back.'

'I found little Star!' said Lucy, taking him out of her pocket to show them. He was still a little damp, but the globe had warmed him so his fur had become very fluffy and he looked very sweet.

'I'm very glad you did,' said Mum. 'But you must never do anything like that again! My goodness Lucy, you could have got so lost out there in the dark and the cold. I can't bear to think of it.'

'I promise I won't do that again, Mum, don't worry,' said Lucy. 'But I was fine, honestly.'

'Only thanks to the magic snow

globe,' she thought.

'You must take the kitten back to the farmer!' said Gran.

'But Gran, can't we keep Star here for just a little bit longer? Until he's properly dry at least,' Lucy asked hopefully, remembering her wish for Star to have a loving home.

'No love, the farmer will be worried. Come on, we can go together,' Gran replied.

They knocked at the farmer's door and the farmer opened it. His face looked very sad until he saw the kitten Lucy was holding out to him.

'Oh, kitten!' he said, taking him in his arms and kissing the top of his head. The kitten purred very loudly. The farmer's face lit up. He got a handkerchief out of his pocket and wiped his eyes.

Lucy was astonished!

'I'm sorry to cry, but I was so worried.

Sounds daft, but he's my little friend, I suppose. I can't thank you enough. You've made my Christmas, you really have,' he said a little awkwardly. 'Please—both of you—come in.'

Lucy was surprised to see that inside the cottage was warm and cosy, not the sort of home she thought a grumpy farmer would have at all. There were no Christmas decorations but there were Christmas cards on the mantelpiece and bright knitted patchwork throws over chairs, and a warm fire, which Star immediately settled in front of. On the walls were photographs of the farmer when he was younger, standing next to a very smiley lady, and others of them with a girl and boy like Lucy and Oscar. The farmer saw Lucy looking at them.

'Those are my children when they were your age. They are all grown up now. That little girl is in America, married with children—look.' He pointed to another photo on the wall of a smiling lady and a man with two toddlers.

'They are beautiful,' said Gran.

'Thank you,' said the farmer, proudly. 'My grandchildren are coming over to visit me in the summer.'

'How lovely,' said Gran, smiling and giving Lucy a hug across her shoulders. 'Grandchildren are so precious.'

'And my son is a vet in Scotland,' said the farmer. 'He's coming over tomorrow.'

The farmer looked at Lucy. 'Thank you very much for finding my kitten, young lady.'

'That's OK,' said Lucy shyly.

'We're delighted he's safe and sound,' said Gran. 'And we love the holiday cottage. Thank you so much, Mr . . . '

'Call me Tom,' said the farmer. 'Tom Loveday.'

'What a beautiful name,' said Gran. 'And I wish you a very happy Christmas!'

'It will be that much better now I've got that little fella home,' said Tom.

'Thanks again.'

Lucy went over to stroke the kitten once more.

'Goodbye little Star,' she said.

'What's that you call him?' said Tom.

'Star, because of that white star he has on his fur,' said Lucy, shyly. She hoped Tom didn't mind.

Tom looked closely and laughed, the first time Lucy had seen his face so smiley. 'You're right! In that case, I will call him Star. My lucky little Star.'

It was hard to say goodbye to such a sweet little kitten, but Lucy knew now that her wish on the snow globe had been granted before she had even made it! Star already had a happy home—he was with the person who loved him most in the whole world. She felt like skipping as she and Gran went back to the cottage.

'I'm so proud of you, Lucy,' said Gran, and gave her a big kiss. 'This is going to be a wonderful Christmas, I know.'

And it was!

Dad and Prajit insisted on Gran judging the baking competition and pretended to get in a huff when she said that Sita's biscuits were the best. Then everybody had hot chocolate and biscuits to warm them up before they went to the Christmas Eve carol service.

On Christmas morning everyone

opened their presents (Sita's grandad had painted lovely pictures of birds for each of them) and the girls and Oscar took Charlie for a walk. They ate a wonderful Christmas dinner, pulled crackers, played board games, and watched TV together.

In the afternoon, Lucy took her present for Star round to Tom's house and he invited her in. She played with Star

and gave him an extra special Christmas cuddle.

'It's been so lovely this holiday,' said Sita, before she went to sleep that night. 'It's been perfect really—snow and kittens and best friends. Happy Christmas, Lucy!'

'Happy Christmas!' said Lucy back. She shook the snow globe so that the

snow fell again over the little cottage in the woods.

'And thank you Snow Globe, for helping me find little Star,' she whispered, and smiled as one of the cottage windows

opened and a little figure in red and a tiny white deer poked their heads out and waved at her.

'Goodnight, Santa, Goodnight, Starlight, Santa's reindeer. Happy Christmas!' Lucy said, and happily thinking of Tom and little Star together again, Lucy fell fast asleep.

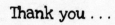

Thank you . . .

Thank you to my lovely agent
Anne Clark.

Thank you very much to everyone
at OUP, especially Liz Cross, Clare
Whitston, and Debbie Sims for their
support for the Lucy books.

Thank you to Sophy Williams for her
beautiful illustrations and to
Sarah Darby for her design.

Love to my husband Graeme and our
children, who are always the first
to hear the Lucy stories, and to all

my encouraging friends. Particular
thanks to the Sole family, who
were with us on holiday when we
rescued a lost kitten and returned
it to a farmer!

I love finding out more about birds
and learnt lots on a tour of the Island
of Lindisfarne organised by Natural
England. I always love watching TV
programmes and reading about birds
too, especially on the RSPB website,
where I read about the hissing sound
the wings of whooper swans make.

About the author

Every Christmas, Anne used to ask for a dog. She had to wait many years, but now she has two dogs, called Timmy and Ben. Timmy is a big, gentle golden retriever who loves people and food and is scared of cats. Ben is a small brown and white cavalier King Charles spaniel who is a bit like a cat because he curls up in the warmest places and bosses Timmy about. He snuffles and snorts quite a lot and you can tell what he is feeling by the way he walks. He has a particularly pleased patter when he has stolen something he shouldn't have, which gives him away immediately. Anne lives in a village in Kent and is not afraid of spiders.

In the story Lucy and Sita make Christmas decorations out of pine cones, and you can too! Turn the page for instructions for making a pine cone owl.

Pine cone owl

What you will need:

Pine cone
Felt
Googly eyes
Craft glue
Scissors
An adult assistant

First you need to prepare your
pine cone, to get rid of the
sap and any bugs that may be
living inside.

What to do

1. Add half a cup of white vinegar to a washing up bowl of warm water.

2. Soak your pine cones for half an hour.

3. After soaking, rinse in fresh water.

4. Choose somewhere that your pine cones can dry, and lay some newspaper down—they will need to be undisturbed for 3-4 days.

5. Put the pine cones down in a single layer.

6. They will probably close up tight when they're washed. When fully dry, the cones will open up.

Once you have a clean, dry pine cone, you're ready to turn it into an owl!

1. Cut a small piece of felt into a number eight shape.

2. Glue googly eyes on—this is your owl's face!

3. Glue the face onto the upper half of the pine cone.

4. Cut a piece of felt into a square—this will be your owl's ears.

5. Glue one of the corners of the square between the owl's eyes, and the opposite corner to the back of the owl's head.

6. Cut a small piece of felt into a triangle—this is your owl's beak.

7. Glue the beak just underneath the googly eyes.

8. Cut a piece of felt into two wings.

9. Glue the wings either side of your owl's body.

10. Cut a piece of felt into two feet.

11. Glue the feet to the lower half of your pine cone.

12. Sit him on a branch of your Christmas tree!

Alternatively, you could glue a loop of string to the top of your owl's head, so that he can hang from the tree.

If you enjoyed

Lucy's Search
for Little Star

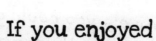

then read on for a taster

of another of Lucy's festive

adventures,

Lucy's Magical
Surprise

ANNE BOOTH

A new arrival...
just in time
for Christmas.

Lucy's Magical
SURPRISE

Illustrated by Sophy Williams

Chapter One

It was the first afternoon of the Christmas
holidays. Lucy and her friends, Rosie and
Sita, were helping out at Lucy's Gran's
Wildlife Rescue Centre, cleaning out the
cages. It was hard work, but it was good

to know that all the animals that were there—six little hedgehogs, a squirrel with a bad foot, and a blackbird with a broken wing—would be comfortable and clean. Lucy helped her Gran out every weekend all year round, and she even had a special red sweatshirt she wore as her uniform. She was very proud to wear it today as she showed her best friends what to do.

'I love all the badges your Gran has made for your uniform,' said Sita. 'One for every type of animal you have helped. I remember the first one she made you for little Bub, the rabbit, the Christmas I first came here from Australia.'

'Now you've got a magpie, a newt, a rabbit, and a hedgehog on this arm,' said Rosie.

'And there's a baby otter on this one,' said Lucy. 'I can't believe that was last Christmas. He was very sweet but very naughty! It was so good we found him a place at the otter sanctuary. Gran and I went to see him learning to swim and he made such a lot of noise!'

'I'll have to make you lots more badges for all the animals you've helped this year, Lucy,' said Gran, coming in from the kitchen. 'I'm a bit behind on my embroidery! The trouble is, the wild animals come in faster than I can make badges. I wish they could live in a safer world. But there's not much we can do about that. So we just have to help them as best as we can. And I don't know what I'd do without you, Lucy, I really don't.'

Lucy gave her Gran a big hug. Apart from playing with Sita and Rosie, looking after animals and birds was her favourite thing to do, and she had lots of books about them. She loved reading them in bed, her little cat Merry and her pyjama-case dog Scruffy tucked up beside her, and her rocking horse Rocky looking on.

Gran looked at the clean cages and floor, and smiled at the three friends.

'My goodness, you have all worked

extremely hard today. Thank you so much! Why don't you wash your hands and then sit down and have some juice and the Christmas biscuits Lucy made me.'

The girls came and sat down in Gran's cosy kitchen. She had Christmas

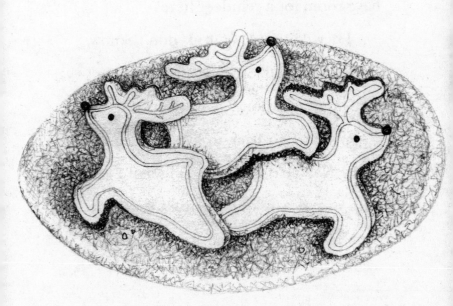

cards and decorations up all over the house, and Christmas carols were playing in the background.

'These are yummy, Lucy!' said Rosie, eating one of the biscuits. 'And I like the reindeer shape!'

'Now, that's a badge you haven't got!' said Gran, smiling. 'I don't think we'd have room for a reindeer here!'

Lucy laughed. 'Oh I don't know, Gran!' she said. 'A baby one wouldn't take up much room!'

'When I go back to live in Australia in the New Year, I'm going to see if I can help out at a wildlife centre,' said Sita. 'I'm hoping there will be koalas and kangaroos there. Maybe I'll even help a joey!'

'What's a joey?' said Lucy.

'It's a baby kangaroo,' said Sita.

'We're going to miss you so much,' said Lucy, suddenly feeling sad. 'I can't believe you are going.'

'I'll miss you too,' said Sita quietly.

'Well, we were lucky to have her and her family for two years,' said Gran. 'And don't forget the puppy Sita is getting in the New Year!'

All the girls brightened up. Ever since they had known Sita was finally going home, they had been talking about the puppy her mum and dad had promised her when they got back to their house in Australia.

'I'll send you lots of pictures!' said Sita. 'I can't wait to collect her—I am going to teach her to sit and fetch and roll over, and we'll go for walks by the beach. She will miss home, the way I did when I came here, but I'll take her to puppy parties and she'll make new friends, like I did you.'

'Hey! We're not puppies!' said Lucy.

'I think it is lovely that your mum and stepdad have moved you all into your grandad's farm, Rosie,' said Gran. 'How exciting that this will be your first Christmas there! Your grandad must be so happy.'

'Yes,' said Rosie. 'When he got ill he couldn't look after it very well, so he is glad we have taken over now. He is coming to stay for Christmas, after the concert at the old people's home.'

'I hope you are singing again this year,' said Gran. 'You have such a lovely voice, Rosie.'

'Yes, I'm singing a carol about a little donkey,' said Rosie.

'And we're seeing Pixie the donkey tomorrow!' said Lucy. 'I can't wait!'

That night Lucy snuggled up in bed and sleepily watched the light from

her Christmas snow globe lamp. She
thought about all the animals she and
Gran had helped in the past year. Lucy

felt sad that so many had been hurt, but glad that they had helped them. Lucy reached over and shook the lamp gently so that the snow fell on the little house in the wood. It was so pretty. She had had it for as long as she could remember, and she always imagined that there was something magic about it, but somehow she didn't know exactly why she thought that. It was as if she had dreamt about it but couldn't recall what was in the dreams.

'I'm sure if any animals live in your wood they are safe and happy,' Lucy said to the snow globe. She settled down in bed, cuddling Scruffy her pyjama case, her little cat Merry purring beside her. Rocky her rocking horse looked down with his kind eyes shining as the moonlight peeped though the curtains, and Lucy closed her eyes and fell fast asleep.

So she didn't see that, for a moment, the snow falling in the globe had turned all the different colours of the rainbow, sparkling blue and red and orange and green and yellow and purple, and there was a distant sound of tinkling bells.

TENGAL
THE FRILLED SHARK

With special thanks to Benjamin Scott

For my late friend Anthony Vivis

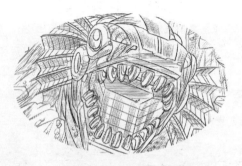

www.seaquestbooks.co.uk

ORCHARD BOOKS
Carmelite House
50 Victoria Embankment
London EC4Y 0DZ

A Paperback Original
First published in Great Britain in 2015

Series created by Beast Quest Limited, London

Text © Beast Quest Limited 2015
Cover and inside illustrations by Artful Doodlers,
with special thanks to Bob and Justin © Orchard Books 2015

A CIP catalogue record for this book is available from
the British Library.

ISBN 978 1 40833 481 2

1 3 5 7 9 10 8 6 4 2

Printed and bound by CPI Group (UK) Ltd, Croydon, CR0 4YY

The paper and board used in this book are made from wood
from responsible sources.

Orchard Books is an imprint of Hachette Children's Group
and published by The Watts Publishing Group Limited,
an Hachette UK company.

www.hachette.co.uk

TENGAL
THE FRILLED SHARK

BY ADAM BLADE

ORCHARD

SIBORG'S HIVE LOG

DESTINATION: AQUORA

A plague is coming to Aquora!

Max and that pathetic Merryn girl
think they have defeated me, but
I have only become stronger. I
have analysed Max's weakness —
his love for his family! And soon
I will take from him all that he
holds dear.

I will do something my weak
father, the so-called Professor,
never could. Take over Aquora! And
I won't even need to fire a single
shot. The city will be mine, and
everyone in it my slaves!

Max couldn't have dreamt up the
horror I have in store for him,
even in his worst nightmares...

CHAPTER ONE

A DIFFICULT INVITATION

Max powered his aquafly through the ocean above rippling coral sands. Large blue-grey anemones poked out of the seabed, their brightly coloured tentacles feeding in the current. Tiny fish pulsing with neon light darted between the flickering strands, snatching specks of food from the anemones' reach. It was a beautiful sight, but Max couldn't enjoy it.

"Where exactly are we going?" he asked the

Professor, who was sitting in the co-pilot's seat.

"To my secret lab, like I told you," his uncle answered. "Just do as I say, and I'll give you further directions when we're in the right sector."

The Professor took out a screwdriver and began poking behind one of the sub's control panels.

"Hey, watch what you're doing with that!" said Max, eyeing his uncle suspiciously. Max had built the sleek aquafly submarine himself, and he knew that it was one of the most advanced vessels in the ocean. All the same, the Professor seemed determined to find something wrong with it.

His uncle yanked out a cluster of wires. "Another amateurish mistake," he said, waving the tangle of red and yellow striped wires around. "You should have connected these to a separate weapons system."

Max's face flushed with anger as he tried to ignore the Professor. He was proud of the aquafly, whatever his uncle said. It could travel below water and over its surface. But what made it special was its hover function. By firing the thrusters downwards the aquafly could fly through the air. In fact, that so-called 'amateurish' technology was the only reason they'd escaped Aquora. The rest of the citizens hadn't been so lucky. They were still under the control of Max's evil half-robotic cousin, Siborg.

"Has the Professor explained where we're heading?" Lia asked over the communicator. Max saw the Merryn princess surge to a stop in the dark waters ahead of the sub, riding her pet swordfish, Spike. She turned back towards them, her silver hair streaming behind her. Max's robodog Rivet floated beside them, his paw rotors whirring.

Max shook his head. "No, he hasn't." He glanced at his uncle, who was busily dismantling another system. Max had to admit the Professor had done a pretty amazing job destroying Siborg's lab-ship, the *Hive*. And without him they would never have escaped with one of the mindbugs Siborg was using to control all the humans of Aquora. But that didn't make it any easier working with him. It wasn't long ago that the Professor's Robobeasts had been feared across Nemos, and it was only thanks to Max that he hadn't taken over the oceans.

He might be our only hope of saving Aquora, Max thought, *but can we trust him?*

The Professor was running his hands over the rim of the drive unit. "Perhaps I should look at the engines. The whole craft seems a bit slow, if you ask me. I hope you didn't

spend too long building this, Max. It would be rather embarrassing if you did."

Max could feel his cheeks getting redder. "My father was impressed with my aquafly."

"Your father has been too soft on you. You've got a great mind, but you've lacked the discipline to really apply it."

Max gritted his teeth. There was nothing wrong with his ship or with the way his father had raised him. *What does the Professor know?* he thought angrily. *His son turned himself into Siborg!*

The intercom crackled to life. "He's done just fine without you, Professor," Lia said. She was clearly listening to their conversation through her communications device. "Max must be smarter than you. He defeated all the Robobeasts you sent against him."

Max flashed Lia a smile to thank her for coming to his defence.

His uncle snorted. "Luck," he sneered. He waved his hand about at the cockpit of the aquafly. "This is really just a glorified underwater tin can."

"It can fly," Lia said. "Not too many tin cans can do that!"

"A child's trick," the Professor replied. "A Robobeast takes much more brains and skill to create. You have to combine technology with living creatures, you see."

Lia launched into a speech about how sea creatures weren't there to be used as playthings. The Professor began to argue back, but Max did his best to ignore them both. He didn't need to be convinced that the robotic experiments of Siborg and his uncle were wrong. He glanced at the mindbug sitting in the glass jar above the controls. Even though it was deactivated, with its stiff legs bent in the air, the sight sent a shiver down his spine.

Max rubbed the skin on the back of his neck, where a mindbug just like it had clamped itself, trying to infect him. He had almost been turned into one of his cousin's mindless cybernetic zombies, like most of Aquora's people – but the Merryn Touch had saved him, as well as his mum and the Professor. Somehow, they were immune to the mindbugs' infection. His dad, Callum, wasn't so lucky. Max's stomach twisted at the thought of his father, still in the city, his mind under Siborg's control. *No more than a droid.*

Max huffed out a long breath of air, trying to shake the guilt of having abandoned his parents – and his home city. *I'll be back*, he promised himself. *Just as soon as we work out how to destroy the mindbugs.*

But to do that they had to get to the Professor's old secret lab. It turned out that Max's uncle had been developing his own tech-disrupting weapons, which meant that he was the only one who had a way to destroy Siborg's mind-control devices.

"Max!" Lia said sharply, interrupting his thoughts. "What do you think?"

Max blinked. Lia was riding Spike close to the aquafly, her gills flaring with anger.

"Think about what?" he asked.

"Who can navigate the sea better?" she demanded. "Me or the Professor?"

"This is ridiculous," the Professor said. "My nav systems can map every millimetre of the seabed!"

"I can read currents with my eyes shut," Lia replied. "Max, I wouldn't trust him not to lead us into a trap."

The Professor put his hand on his heart in mock outrage. "That hurts!" he said. "We're family."

How has it come to this – being on the same side as my evil uncle? Max wondered. *I never thought I'd be working with him to save Aquora!*

Max sighed. "We don't have a choice, Lia."

His friend surged forward on Spike. "Just keep an eye on him," she said angrily.

"I assure you, if I wanted you dead you

would be," the Professor snapped. He pointed at Lia, darting in the water just outside the sub. "My weapons are more than a match for any Merryn…"

Here they go again, Max thought. If only his dad was here – he'd have straightened them out in seconds.

Lia was already shouting back through the communications device, when the aquafly vid-screen flickered into life. Max held his breath. *It can't be.* A grainy image of his dad appeared on the screen.

Max hesitated. "Dad?" The last time they'd spoken, Callum was under Siborg's control and had arrested him.

Callum's eyes were wide, his mouth open in panic. But his shoulders sagged with relief when he saw Max. "Son, thank Nemos you're alive! I can't talk for long. I've managed to escape Siborg's control. I've fled in a sub."

He held up what looked like a submarine's tracking unit. "I've managed to…" The speakers hissed with interference. The image rolled with waves of static.

"…meet me?" Callum said, reappearing on the vid-screen. "Sending you coordinates for the outskirts of the Forest of Souls. We should be safe from Siborg there." Callum's face dissolved into wavy lines before the screen went blank.

Max's heart raced as he quickly punched the coordinates into the nav system. They weren't far off! He couldn't wait to see his father again – with Callum's help, he was sure they could defeat Siborg. Max reached for the steering column. "Next stop, the Forest of Souls!"

CHAPTER TWO

RETURN TO THE FOREST OF SOULS

The Professor grabbed Max's hands away from the controls. "You're an idiot if you fall for this," he said. "It's clearly another of Siborg's tricks, and a rather flimsy one at that. Your father can't have disabled the mindbug on his own."

"Why can't you just accept that he's escaped?" snapped Max, as he jerked free of the Professor's grip. "You always underestimate my family. Perhaps Mum used her immunity to the mindbugs to help free my dad. She's probably with him, waiting for me!"

Lia cleared her throat. "Max, even if the Professor isn't completely right, it's too dangerous to go to those coordinates. What if Siborg deliberately let your dad go to track him? We'd be heading straight into Siborg's snare."

"I can't just ignore my dad when he says he's escaped," Max said. "Siborg wants to turn him and my mum into his own set of parents. He wouldn't let my father go!"

The Professor groaned. "Dratted emotions getting in the way. Even the dolphin-hugger can see it's a trap!"

Lia scowled at the Professor, but didn't look as though she was going to argue.

"Trap, Max!" barked Rivet.

Max took a deep breath, fighting to control

his emotions. Lia was just looking out for him, but he couldn't simply ignore Callum's message. "What if instead of heading straight for the Forest of Souls we find a sneakier route?" he said. "Then we can make sure it's not a trap before we meet him."

Max checked the nav-charts and then pointed out of the watershield to a network of ravines criss-crossing the seabed. They led all the way up to the edge of the kelp forest, in the distance. "These will keep us hidden from any radar or scanners. Happy?"

"Hardly." The Professor crossed his arms and shook his head, but Max decided to take that as a 'yes'.

He piloted the aquafly down into an underwater gorge scarring the seabed, followed by Lia, Spike and Rivet. Soon the deep chasm swallowed up the sub and the waters washing over the watershield darkened. Max activated the sub's spotlights and aimed them ahead. Occasionally the dark, flitting shapes of Rivet and Lia riding Spike were suddenly lit up in the aquafly's powerful rays.

There! Max spotted a rocky opening in the wall of the gorge. He spoke to Lia through his mic. "Follow me!"

"Last chance to turn back," grumbled the Professor from beside him. Max ignored his uncle and plunged the craft through the dark entrance. Purple starfish scuttled across the crumbling red stone walls. Huge octopuses darted into tiny holes, hiding from the aquafly's bright lights.

Max swerved down another tunnel. "Hold on," he said as he tipped the aquafly on its side. They shot through a tight gap. Max righted the craft and concentrated on keeping the sub's wings from clipping the rocks.

They had been going for a while when,

finally, Max glimpsed the vast expanse of kelp that was the Forest of Souls between two craggy walls, ahead. They had reached the end of the ravine network. He eased back on the throttle as they exited the tunnel. "Keep an eye out for signs of an ambush," said Max to the others, as he gazed at the forest below.

"Rivet keep watch, Max," said his dogbot.

Huge towers of seaweed rose from the ocean floor like trees, their feathery fronds creating a dark, wavering carpet. Max scanned the canopy but couldn't see any sign of Siborg.

He accelerated across the short gap into the forest with Lia, Spike and Rivet close behind. He brightened the aquafly's headlights, but they didn't penetrate far into the dense kelp forest.

"Rivet, activate lamps," he ordered.

"Yes, Max," Rivet barked, and bright beams of light shone from his eyes. Max searched the oceans for Callum's ship. Part of him kept expecting to see the massive robotic shape of Siborg's battle suit emerge from the gloom, or the horrific glint of his cousin's glowing red eye. *Come on, Dad…* Max thought.

There was something creepy about this place. A memory returned to him – fighting Manak the Silent Predator in these murky depths. Manak was one of the Professor's early Robobeasts, and had almost killed Lia. Max swallowed and wondered what other terrors lurked in the Forest of Souls.

"My dad must have decided this was a good place to hide from Siborg," Max murmured, trying to reassure himself.

"Or Siborg thinks it's a good place to trap us," the Professor said. "Don't use the radio in case it gives away our position."

"Max!" Lia's worried voice came through his comms device. "Look!"

A cold finger traced a line down Max's spine as he saw a dark, hovering shape in a clearing ahead.

Max nosed the aquafly through the giant seaweed towards the edge of the circular clearing. As they got closer, he could see a large Hunter Class Aquoran sub floating in the middle. He felt a surge of hope. "It must

be Dad!" Max said.

"Then why isn't he trying to contact us?" asked the Professor.

"Maybe he's lost communications," said Max. The Aquoran vessel was alone, but its grey surface was battered with black scorch marks and blaster bolt dents.

"It's been in a fight," Lia said. "Perhaps Siborg tried to stop it from escaping."

Max scanned the viewing ports for clues, and spotted a figure behind the ship's watershield. *Dad!* He was alone on the bridge.

Max flashed his headlights, and Callum peered out and grinned. Max gave the thumbs up, buzzing with joy at the sight of his father. Callum reached for some controls before pointing to the sub's loading bay doors. They opened.

"See, nothing to worry about," Max said. "Siborg would have had a Robobeast or an army of cyrates in there to capture us!"

"You still might want to blast his thrusters first," the Professor advised. "Stop him getting away."

Max shook his head. "I'm not going to open fire on my dad, no matter what happens." He guided the aquafly towards the cargo bay.

As he landed inside, Lia dismounted and swam with Rivet into the bay beside them, securing her Amphibio mask. "Back in a sec," she said to Spike, who was bobbing in the water. The cargo bay doors slid shut in front of the swordfish. Water drained through the holes in the deck as the airlock was re-established. The aquafly rested on the metal floor.

Max was about to release the aquafly's exit hatch when the Professor drew out a blaster. "No weapons," Max said.

The Professor shrugged. "This is your stupid decision, but we need protection."

Max gave a slow nod. *Perhaps he's right.* There was no harm in being prepared. He strapped on his hyperblade, as Lia unslung the spear from her back and twirled it. Even if he didn't want to use the blade against his father, he might have to use it on the Professor.

Rivet leapt over to Max, wagging his tail. "Easy, boy," Max said. "Stay here, guard the aquafly!"

"Yes, Max," the dogbot barked.

Max led Lia and the Professor out of the cargo bay. The corridors were lit with red emergency lighting. *The sub must have taken a beating*, Max thought.

The lifts were out of action, so Max took them up the ladder shaft to the command deck. He reached the airlock door to the bridge and turned to the Professor. "Stay out of sight. If it's a trap I'll call for you."

The Professor narrowed his eyes. "Very well."

Max pressed the bridge door controls, his heart pounding. He couldn't wait to talk to his father and find out what had happened. The door slid open. Max and Lia rushed inside.

His father's normal smart black uniform

had lost its gold braid and was ripped in places, but his face lit up when he saw Max. "It's so good to see you safe, and Lia too!" His voice sounded full of emotion – nothing like someone controlled by a mindbug. Callum ran forward and swept Max up in a big hug.

Lia stepped away from Callum's reach. "What's the matter?" Max asked.

"He might still be under Siborg's control," Lia whispered, clutching her spear tight.

Max pulled himself out of his dad's embrace, staring him in the face. "Dad, how did you escape?"

"My mindbug malfunctioned," Callum said. "So I removed it." He folded down his collar. The mindbug was gone. It had left a circle of red marks around an angry, puckered scar.

Max turned to Lia, but his smile faded as he saw her step back. She didn't take her eyes off Callum. Max knew she had good reason to be cautious, but his father was clearly back to his old self. "How about this?" he said. "If he can answer questions that only my dad would know, we'll be sure he's not Siborg's control."

The Merryn girl nodded as Callum frowned. "What sort of questions?"

"Dad, what was the first piece of technology I helped reprogramme?"

Callum hesitated then smiled. "You helped fix the climate controls in the apartment.

Except it went a bit wrong…you boosted the air conditioning so much it blew out snow!"

Max grinned as he remembered the white powder streaming around their living room. "And when did you buy me Rivet?"

Callum narrowed his eyes. "That's a trick question, you built him yourself."

"Both correct," Max said. He turned to Lia. "I don't think he'd be able to answer those if he was in Siborg's power."

Lia nodded, smiling behind her Amphibio mask. "I agree."

"Dad, what's happening in Aquora?" Max said. "Where's Mum?"

"Siborg is still in control," Callum replied, looking worried. "Niobe has been locked up. Siborg still hasn't managed to make a mindbug that can infect someone with the Merryn Touch, but he's working on it."

He suddenly reached for his side-arm and

pointed it over Max's shoulder. "What are you doing here? I should arrest you at once!"

Max spun around. The Professor was standing on the bridge. He was glaring at Callum, his hand on his blaster.

"Stand back, Max!" his dad said.

"Wait!" Max pushed Callum's pistol away. "The Professor is on our side. You can't arrest him. His secret lab has the technology to build a weapon that will take out the mindbugs. It's Aquora's only hope."

All life dropped from his father's face. His eyes dulled and his mouth looked expressionless. "Thank you, Max." A robotic voice came from his mouth. "That's just what I wanted to know."

A vid-screen lit up on a wall behind him and Siborg's half-robotic face grinned out at them.

Max's heart sank.

It was a trap all along!

CHAPTER THREE

A NARROW ESCAPE

Siborg swept his brown hair away from the riveted metal plating and robotic implants to reveal his glowing red eye. It flicked over Max and across the bridge. His human eye had a glint of victory as it stared out of the vid-screen straight at Max. *He can't have beaten us already!*

"But he no longer had a mindbug!" Max exclaimed.

Siborg laughed. "Yes, I removed the

original mindbug, and replaced it with a better concealed device on his lower back. Soon I won't even need that one. Once a victim has been infected, it's not long before the infection becomes permanent, and the bug itself is no longer needed."

Max's father flinched and felt for the new mindbug. His eyes widened as he touched it. "But…but…I remember escaping," Callum stuttered, in his own voice. "I…I was free of that monster!"

"Of course you did. Max wouldn't have been fooled if I had made contact. It had to be you." Siborg smirked. "And I had to free your mind, so Max wouldn't be suspicious. You were easy enough to track and take control of again when I wanted."

Max's cheeks flushed with anger. Siborg was toying with them all, using his father like a plaything. "Wait until we find out how to disrupt your mind control tech!"

"Time is running out for that," Siborg replied. "Very soon my infections will become permanent."

"Son, perhaps we could talk about this," the Professor said, stepping forward.

Siborg's manic grin vanished. "No! Your time is up." The vid-screen went blank.

A flash of light from outside caught Max's eye. Something metallic had reflected off the submarine's search beams.

"What's that?" Lia asked.

Max ran to the watershield, his father and the Merryn princess crowding next to him.

"Can you see anything?" Callum asked, putting his hands on their shoulders.

Max pointed to a rippling patch of seaweed. He swung the sub's headlights towards the kelp and caught a gigantic pair of grey, robotic eyes. The creature they belonged to pushed through the kelp to reveal a massive, torpedo-shaped head. It surged forward, showing a long tapered body made of overlapping metal plates. "It's some sort of robotic sea serpent," Max gasped.

"Wrong. In fact it's a frilled shark." Siborg's voice rattled over the speakers. "Meet my

newest Robobeast, Tengal. His mouth is the last thing you're ever going to see."

The creature opened its jaws wide to reveal rows and rows of jagged metal teeth. They whirled rapidly, turning the mouth into a giant electric grinder. The Robobeast snapped at a massive trunk of seaweed, instantly turning the water deep green as the plant was liquidised.

Tengal snaked away from the kelp, curling its body before shooting straight at them. Max gripped the console as the frilled shark smashed headfirst into the sub only a few decks below. *Bang!*

A shockwave ripped through the bridge, knocking Max from his feet. He lay sprawled against the deck next to Lia and his father. The lights flickered and sparks erupted from one of the control panels.

Max scrambled up and pressed himself

against the watershield to see if Tengal had been damaged. Lia ran beside him and scanned the water. "Spike!" she shouted. Luckily the swordfish was out of sight.

Max watched as the Robobeast swept away, its huge metal head not even dented. He reached out to help his father, but Callum was already up, striding away to the escape pod. "Where are you going?" Max shouted. He tried to grab his father's arm, but Callum pushed him away. Max looked into his dad's face and felt a jolt of horror. It was blank once more.

"That's right – come home, Father," Siborg called. "We will rule Siborgia together!"

The sound of a blaster charging up jerked Max around. The Professor had his weapon aimed at Callum. "We can't just let him escape, you fool!" he yelled. "He's not getting the only escape pod."

"Don't!" Max grabbed the Professor's hand and shook the blaster from his grip. "You're just out for yourself!"

"So what?" The Professor pushed Max away, trying to reach down for the blaster. "It's a fish eat fish world down here."

Max tackled the Professor. He grabbed his legs and tried to pull them from under him. The Professor beat his fist against Max's back.

Callum slammed the escape pod shut.

"See what you've done," snarled the Professor.

A deep rumble erupted from behind the hatch. Max squirmed free of his uncle and sprinted to the watershield, looking out into the ocean. A sphere of some tough alloy blasted out above the bridge. His father's escape pod shot up over the clearing and across the kelp forest, faster and faster.

Max looked round for Tengal, picturing its grinding teeth ripping the pod to shreds. But the frilled shark was nowhere to be seen. Max followed the orb carrying his father, as it disappeared into the darkness.

"I'm sorry." Lia touched Max's shoulder, but before she could say anything else she gasped. Tengal reared out of a gap in the kelp, its massive head – half-snake, half-shark – looming before them for a moment. Then it rammed into the side of the Aquoran vessel

once again. A shockwave surged through the control deck. Max felt his feet swept from under him. He crashed to the steel floor of the bridge, Lia and the Professor sprawling beside him.

"Watch out!" shouted Lia. Max threw his arms over his head as ceiling panels, lights and ducting crashed around them. He could hear sparking from the control panel and the creaking of bending metal. *The hull is going to be breached!*

Max scrambled up. Tengal's plated body was rippling as it swung around to batter them again. Max knew from his father that Hunter Class submarines were equipped with the latest Aquoran weapons. He ran to the weapon systems and jabbed his fingers at a combination of buttons. "What are you doing?" shouted the Professor.

"I'm trying to activate the missile sensors,"

Max called back.

Max flicked the final switch. Nothing. Not a single light glowed on the control panel. Max flicked the switch again. Still nothing. He slammed the side of the controls, but the weapons systems were dead. *Siborg must have disabled them*, Max realised. They were completely defenceless.

He grabbed Lia and ran towards the Professor. "Time to get out of here," he shouted. "Back to the aquafly!"

As they reached the bridge doors, Max glanced back. Rows of spinning teeth filled the view from the watershield as Tengal smashed into the bridge. Max threw his arms against the wall to stop himself from being thrown to the floor as the sub shook again. Lia had caught the stumbling Professor. "Quick," Max gasped, "before it punctures the hull."

Making sure the Professor and Lia kept up, Max slid down the ladder and skidded into the cargo bay. *Bang!* The submarine shuddered again and the creaking got louder. Max caught the edge of a crate to stop himself from being knocked down. Rivet jumped up, barking. "What is it, Max?"

"Another Robobeast, Rivet," Max told him as he opened up the aquafly.

"Wait," the Professor panted. "Your craft is nothing against Tengal."

Max ignored the Professor and pushed him into the aquafly, followed by Rivet. He hurried in behind and sealed the door. Checking the controls, Max flicked the switch to release the cargo bay doors.

A warning message flashed up on the aquafly's vid-screen:

<<DOORS LOCKED>>

Max thumped the control panel.

If the doors were locked, he'd have to find the manual override. He crawled out of the side hatch of the aquafly. "What are you doing, Max?" Rivet whined. But Max was already gone.

"Back in a moment!" he called back. He sprinted towards the large control panel at the side of the cargo bay doors and jabbed at them furiously. The creaking inside the cargo bay was deafening now. *Come on!* But the panel was as lifeless as the controls on the bridge.

Boom! Another shock wave trembled through the cargo bay. The deck felt as though it was sliding out from under them. Max grabbed hold of a metal box next to the panel to stop himself from falling. It had something written on it, but was covered in a layer of dirt. He wiped it with his hand. Lia was beside him. "What is it?"

"Cargo bay door release," Max read aloud.

He tried to open it, but someone had welded it shut. Siborg. Max scanned the cargo bay for something to break it open with. Then he caught sight of his dogbot through the screen of the aquafly. "Rivet, come here," he shouted.

Rivet bounded from the sub and charged over, his stubby tail wagging.

"Hold still," Max ordered. He slid open the control panel behind the dogbot's head and quickly redirected the energy supply to Rivet's jaw. *This should make him able to bite through anything.* Max slid the panel back.

"Rivet, bite!"

Rivet growled as his jaws clenched around the metal box, ripping it from the wall. Sparks flew from switches inside and red lights flashed into action around the cargo bay. "Manual door release override," a computerised voice warned.

"You did it, Rivet!" cried Lia.

Airlocks around the cargo bay slammed open and water bubbled up from the deck. Max splashed towards his aquafly. The water rose rapidly. Lia's hair was already floating around her, and she pulled off her Amphibio mask. As soon as the cargo bay pressure equalised, the doors would open. *Then we*

have to face Tengal, Max thought.

Max swam the last few metres to the aquafly and climbed in. As he crawled to his seat, a loud mechanical groaning rang out across the bay and the doors began to slide apart. "Nice of you to join me," said the Professor. He pointed ahead. "Just in time to be ripped to shreds by a Robobeast."

The dark ocean of the Forest of Souls opened out beyond the cargo doors. Max looked down, activating the aquafly's weapons: acid torpedoes, powerful blasters... But a gasp from Lia made him look up.

A colossal arrow-like head was careering straight towards them. Huge grey eyes stared at them from between metal plating, and teeth like hyperblades glinted in the gloom.

Tengal.

CHAPTER FOUR

TENGAL'S SECRET WEAPON

Bang! Tengal's pointed nose rammed the gap between the bay doors. Max gripped the controls as the aquafly was jolted across the submerged cargo bay. The sub's lights flickered and went out.

Max activated the aquafly's headlamps. The edges of the metal doors were buckled where the Robobeast had smashed into them.

Whirrrrrrr!

Tengal ripped more pieces off with its

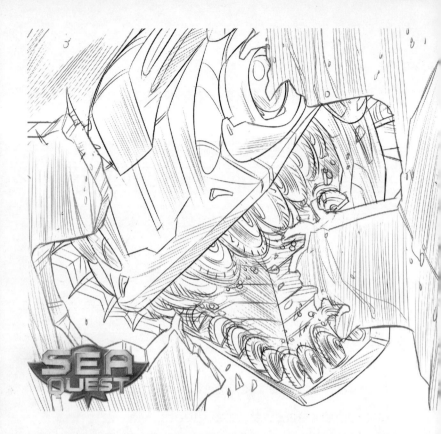

grinding teeth, but the gap still wasn't wide enough to let the frilled shark inside the sub.

"We're cornered," said Lia, through her communicator.

The Robobeast swerved away, giving Max a flash of its long rippling body. *Thud!* Its side hit the doors, creating a snaking indentation.

"If we don't do something it's either going

to pulverise us, or trap us in a sinking sub," the Professor yelled.

"We're going to have to make a run for it," Max replied, clicking on the communicator. "Lia, grab on so we don't lose you. Rivet, engage full power. Follow us closely."

Lia scrambled to the wing and clutched its front edge. Max lined the aquafly up with the gap in the cargo bay doors. They couldn't open any wider, but the gap was just big enough for their escape. *It's going to be a tight squeeze though*, Max thought.

He slammed on the thrusters. The engines roared into life, and the aquafly shot towards the gap. Max gripped the steering column firmly, keeping his eyes on the exact middle of the opening. With a nudge to the right, the aquafly burst out into the murky water without even a scrape on it.

"Nice work, Max," yelled Lia.

Max twisted around, looking for Tengal. He couldn't see where the Robobeast had got to. "Spike!" Lia called. The swordfish tore through the water until he was close enough for Lia to slide onto his back.

Suddenly, Tengal barrelled out of the kelp forest at them, its body rippling. Max swerved away, narrowly missing its whirring teeth. He looked to the side of the aquafly, relieved to see Rivet swimming through the water. Max looked down into a screen displaying an image from the rear-view camera.

"Whoa!" Max cried. The Robobeast was right behind them. The next moment it rammed into the submarine, tearing a massive chunk from its side and releasing an explosion of air bubbles.

"Max, we should run while we have the chance," Lia urged over the comms. "We're easy targets out here."

"You don't say," muttered the Professor.

"Rivet. Lia. This way!" Max powered the aquafly towards the thick forest of kelp at the nearest edge of the clearing. They might be able to lose Tengal there.

In the rear-view screen, Max spotted that the frilled shark had dropped back and was coiled over the wrecked Aquoran submarine. Its eyes seemed to burn with hunger. *What's it doing?* Suddenly, it flicked its long body and leapt forward, propelling itself at incredible speed. But as it arrowed through the water, Max realised that the Robobeast wasn't heading after them. "No!" he cried.

Rivet was halfway between the aquafly and the sub, and Tengal was charging after him. The dogbot was moving more slowly than normal – too slowly to escape.

"A jet-thruster failure," the Professor mused. *Rivet's propulsion systems must have been damaged when I rerouted power to his jaws,* Max realised.

Foam poured from Tengal's mouth as its grinders churned up the water. If Rivet got caught in the Robobeast's teeth, then there would be nothing left of him for Max to repair.

"Faster, Rivet," Max called over the comms.

"Can't go faster, Max," Rivet whined.

The Robobeast surged closer. Max wrenched the aquafly's steering and pitched the sub sharply towards the dogbot. He pushed the throttle to maximum power. He wasn't going to let Tengal tear Rivet apart.

"What are you doing?" the Professor cried.

"Saving him," Max snapped, flicking on the comms. "Rivet, magnetise your paws!"

He jammed the aquafly into a tight U-turn to get as close to Rivet as he could. *Clunk!* Rivet's feet clamped onto the wing. "Good boy," called Max.

He punched the engines' boost button. But instead of jetting through the water the aquafly juddered to a halt. A loud whirring noise reverberated around the cockpit, and with horror, Max felt the sub being pulled backwards. He looked behind them. Tengal's mouth was open, twice as large as the aquafly. Bubbles churned in circles around the Robobeast's mouth. Water and bits of seaweed were being sucked, swirling, down into its throat. *It must be creating a vacuum-like force*, Max realised. The current from the beast's mouth was dragging the aquafly quicker and quicker towards the sharp rotating teeth.

"Ah," said the Professor. "A high-powered suction weapon. Ingenious!"

Max jabbed frantically at the controls, trying to divert as much power to the engines as he could. It made no difference – they were still heading backwards.

Tengal's jaws clamped down around the back of the aquafly. A metallic squeal filled Max's ears. Judders shook through him as the side panels buckled and twisted.

"Do something," the Professor demanded. "Before it tears through the sub!"

"Max!" Lia called over the comms. "Remember the depth charges!"

"Good idea!" Max aimed the weapons at the back of the frilled shark's mouth where the jaws were hinged together. "Try eating this!" he yelled.

He fired the depth charges. Six black canisters popped from the aquafly into the churning water around the grinders, sucked downwards. Max braced himself.

BOOM! A massive explosion lit up the Robobeast's mouth and a shockwave blasted its jaws open, throwing Max and the Professor forward and flinging the aquafly into the kelp forest. Max wrestled with the steering. As the aquafly slowed, he finally regained control. The Professor pointed out of the watershield at some algae-covered rocks. "Go down there and hide from Tengal."

Max nodded. "Riv, Lia, to me!" He took the aquafly down into the thickest part of the seaweed. Max caught sight of the Robobeast in the rear-view screen. It was thrashing around, damaged from the blast. Easing the steering stick downwards, Max tucked his vessel between two slime-covered boulders. He shut off the engines.

Lia and Spike nestled down next to them, and Rivet pawed at the plexiglass. "Big monster, Max."

You can say that again, Riv.

Max flicked the exit hatch switch and heard his dogbot enter the airlock. There was a whoosh of draining water and then Rivet crawled into the cockpit beside him, nuzzling up to him. "It's okay, Rivet," Max whispered, patting his dogbot.

Lia swam closer through the dark fronds of seaweed outside. "Do you think we're safe?"

"Hopefully," Max murmured. Tengal had disappeared. Maybe he'd gone back to Siborg for repairs.

"Of course, if I had designed this vessel we would have had enough advanced weaponry to destroy the Robobeast," the Professor said. "We won't be truly safe until we get to my lab."

"What about my dad?" Max said. "Shouldn't we go after his escape pod?"

"If my son was telling the truth about the infection becoming permanent, going after Callum will only delay us," replied the Professor. "And that time could be vital to stopping the mindbug control."

Max stared into the dark green forest of seaweed and shadows. He nodded reluctantly. He hated to admit it, but stopping the mindbug infection was more important than having his father close by. Max peered through the swaying kelp to the clearing. Tengal was nowhere to be seen. He revved the engines. "You'd better show us the way to your secret lab then, Professor."

CHAPTER FIVE

THE HOWLING CAVES

Max pushed the aquafly through the Forest of Souls, steering around gigantic stalks of seaweed. Their dark green fronds were getting caught in the thrusters. Churning sounds kept coming from below the cockpit. The Professor raised an eyebrow at his nephew but Max ignored him, fighting to keep the aquafly level as the engines protested.

The Professor tapped the sub's display and cleared his throat. "Not looking good."

Max saw that the power gauge was registering less than a quarter. He was sure they'd escaped Tengal, but it was too dangerous to emerge from the kelp forest in case Siborg was tracking them.

"Siborg doesn't need to send a Robobeast to kill us," the Professor scoffed. "It's only a matter of time before your ship loses control."

"He's a fool, Max," said Lia through the comms. She darted through the water in front of the struggling sub, holding onto Spike's fin.

Max gritted his teeth. He couldn't stand his uncle's glee at the small craft's problems. "I'll run a systems check."

The Professor waved off the suggestion with a grunt. "If you think that'll help."

Max activated the systems check. Within seconds, the programme flashed up its answer: <<Systems at 30%. Recommendation: clear water from thrusters.>> A glowing green button shone from the touchscreen.

Max pressed it. A groan reverberated around the craft before a blast of water erupted out of the back of the sub's jets, sending the rags of seaweed spiralling away. The aquafly's controls instantly became easier to handle again.

Max pushed the throttle down and was glad to see the giant seaweed trees thinning out. *I hope I never have to come back to the Forest of Souls*, he thought. He checked the ship's navigation maps. "This is further west in the Delta Quadrant than I've ever been," he said.

"Secret bases are best built where nobody goes," his uncle said. "I should have thought that was obvious. My lab is on the very edge of the sector, bordering the Gamma Quadrant."

Max pushed the vessel onwards, staying down close to the sea floor. All signs of life quickly vanished. The seaweed and kelp died out, replaced by rocks and boulders with large stretches of sand between them. It was strange not to see even a single fish, but the temperature gauge was dropping steadily, and the water was turning an eerie green.

Max could see through the watershield that Lia's skin had paled along with the cold ocean and she was shivering. Even Spike had slowed and swam level with the aquafly.

"This may be worse than the Forest of Souls," Max said, as he checked the radar. It was clear behind and above them. "But we should be able to spot Tengal if he follows us."

The Professor tapped the nav-screen map. "If you can manage it without getting lost, take a steady course towards here," he said.

Max bit his tongue and plotted the Professor's course. He felt a chill creep down his spine. He still expected a Robobeast to jump out at them any second. Either Tengal, or perhaps some monster the Professor had planned for them. *He could be leading us into a trap*, Max thought, eyeing his uncle.

Something blipped on the sonar in front of them. It was too large to be a ship. Max's heart hammered as he peered at the eerie green glow he could see in the distance.

Rivet's ears pricked up and he raised his head off Max's lap. "Hear something, Max.

Creature in trouble."

Max turned up the volume on the sea microphones. He could hear a faint wailing ahead. But the sound was too steady for it to be a creature in distress. His sound scanner showed that the noise was coming from the huge mass on the radar.

Max turned the volume down on the microphones as low as they could go, but the wailing pulsed through the watershield in waves of bone-vibrating groans. His head throbbed with it. Oddly, the Professor looked totally calm. *Does he know something I don't?*

Finally a huge outcrop of green rocks came into view, rising out of the ocean floor. Jagged emerald crystals grew out of the stone. *They look sharper than my hyperblade*, thought Max. Openings and tunnels dotted the formation, obviously leading into caves and tunnels within. "The noise must be coming

from there," Max said.

"Of course it must," the Professor replied. "These are the legendary Howling Caves. That groaning is caused by the ghosts of all the sailors who have died inside them."

The thought of haunted caves sent a wave of cold dread through Max, but he was surprised the Professor believed such a tale. *There's got to be a more scientific explanation*, he thought.

"Are you sure it isn't the acoustics of the

tunnel making the sound?" Max said.

The Professor raised an eyebrow, but before he could speak Lia banged on the watershield. "Is your secret base here, Professor?" she yelled over the sound of groaning rocks.

"Don't be ridiculous," the Professor said. "It would be far too dangerous. Not to mention noisy." He sighed. "We've taken a detour because Max was stupid enough to tell Siborg our plans. We needed to shake him off."

Max wondered if the Professor ever had a good word to say about anyone or anything but himself. "The fate of Aquora and my parents is in our hands and we're sightseeing?"

"We needed to come here anyway," his uncle said, raising his voice over the loud humming. "This is the only place we'll find a certain type of crystal that vibrates at the exact frequency necessary to disable the mindbugs. Some Merryn believe the crystals are sacred to Thallos. Superstitious nonsense, of course."

Max's head throbbed with the constant roar of the caverns. He glanced at Lia and Spike outside the window. She didn't seem to have noticed the Professor's insult. "Are you okay, Lia?" he yelled.

She shook her head. "I'm just wondering if we'll need to engage an energy shield before entering the cavern."

Max blinked. Lia had never shown much interest in tech before. He hadn't realised she even knew what an energy shield was. *I guess it was inevitable that the technology bug would bite her,* he thought. He winced as he reminded himself of Siborg's horrific mindbugs.

"We'll be fine without one," the Professor retorted.

Max steered for the largest entrance into the Howling Caves. Spike was squirming and bucking beneath Lia, as though he didn't want to go in. "Is Spike all right?" he asked.

Lia tugged at his dorsal fin. "The stupid fish is spooked about the caves. He'll snap out of it." Lia gave Spike a sharp tap on the side with her hand. "Behave, will you?"

Max shook his head. He'd never heard Lia talk to her pet like that. *The screech of the Howling Caves must really be getting to her.* But his brain ached too from the unbelievable noise made by the vibrating crystals.

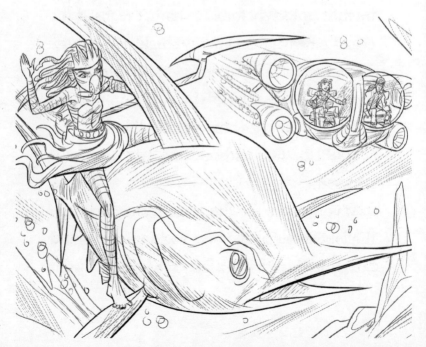

"Shall we go?" the Professor sighed. "Or do you need a moment with your girlfriend?"

Max shot him an angry look and powered the aquafly into the mouth of the cave. As darkness enclosed them, Max flicked on the craft's lights. Thousands of small crystals scattered the lamplight, making the cave glow with green light. The wailing echoed off the walls. It magnified the intensity of the noise battering Max's ears. *I'm going to have to do something before it deafens us all*, Max thought.

He pressed his hand over one ear and reprogrammed the acoustic controls on their communicators. The groans didn't vanish, but the moaning was dampened to a level where he could think clearly again. Max noticed Lia's face and even the Professor's relax a little as their comms activated the acoustic blocking.

"That's better," Max said, looking around the cavern walls. "Now we can grab one of these crystals and go. Take your pick, Professor."

The Professor tutted. "None of these will do. They'll be too fragile and unstable for my plans. We need one grown at the centre of the cave system." He pointed to a tunnel leading downwards, lined with sword-like crystals.

"That's going to take some careful manoeuvring," Max said. The jagged crystals and rocks lining the walls looked as though they would rip the aquafly to pieces.

A jolt ran through Max as the craft bucked suddenly. "What in Nemos?" he exclaimed. Water shimmered over the plexiglass and across the wings. It threw them forward again.

"Didn't I mention the undertow?" the Professor said. "These caverns are riddled with dangerous currents."

"Now you tell us!" Max yelled. With another jolt, the current rammed the aquafly towards the crystals surrounding the tunnel entrance.

"Three seconds to impact," the Professor said.

The sharp ends of the crystals glinted in the headlights, dangerously close. Max slammed on full reverse. "Come on!"

"Two seconds…"

The aquafly's engines squealed, but he couldn't escape the flow of water. The water buffeted them one way, then another.

"One second…" The Professor threw up his arms to cover his eyes. Rivet whined and cowered beside Max.

Crash! The aquafly smashed against the lip of the tunnel, razor-sharp splinters of crystal flying in all directions. The headlights exploded, plunging them into darkness. The aquafly spun, still dragged by the undertow. Shattered crystal and broken rock scratched against the watershield. *I've completely lost control!* Max thought as they plunged into the roaring depths of the Howling Caves.

CHAPTER SIX

BETRAYAL

"Rivet, lamps on," Max shouted.

The dogbot aimed his beams outside the watershield. The churning white water was lit up before them, along with another crystal formation that the aquafly was swooping towards. *Not again!* Max gripped the steering column. He pressed his foot hard against the brakes, but it didn't help.

The craft smashed into the outcrop. The force of the impact almost threw Max from his seat. He pulled the harness straps tighter.

Rivet's light flashed on the green crystal fragments swirling in the water. The walls of the winding tunnel spun around and around them at dizzying speed as they were dragged through. Max pressed a hand to his mouth to stop himself being sick. *This had better be worth it*, he thought. *If we even survive.*

The craft was moving at colossal speed now. Max hoped Lia and Spike were okay outside.

"Don't worry," said the Professor. "We're going the right wa—" Max slammed into his uncle as the sub was slung around another sharp bend. The force of it launched Rivet into the air. The dogbot yelped in surprise. He slammed against the watershield with a loud smack then rebounded into Max's stomach.

"Oof!" Max moaned. A wave of nausea returned, stronger than ever.

"Sorry, Max," Rivet whined.

The Professor spluttered. "Watch it, boy.

You winded me. Oh look, more problems…"

Warning lights flashed across the aquafly's controls. Max could hear the engines screaming over the roar of the current. The engine's temperature gauge had swung into the red danger zone. Max had no choice but to cut engine power. The craft spun faster through the rapids. *When is this going to end?*

Max steered as best he could using the hydraulic wing-flaps, nudging the aquafly away from the deadly cavern walls that threatened to dash them to pieces.

He saw Lia, gripping Spike with her arms around his neck and her legs wrapped around his dorsal fin. The fierce current whipped up her long silver hair like seaweed in a storm. She looked quite calm. The Professor grabbed Max's arm and pointed up. "Shelter in that crevice before we're ripped apart!" he shouted.

Max nodded, but the current was too strong

for the normal engines. *Perhaps I can use the force of the aquafly's sea-to-air jump-thrusters to give us a boost*, he thought.

He activated the controls, and with a roar they shot out of the undertow straight into the narrow slit between the hard rocks. Sparks flew off the wings as they scraped against the crevice walls and the craft slowed to a halt.

Outside, Max spotted Lia clinging to Spike's back. He let out a sigh of relief. "That was close," Max shouted over the roaring water.

"We can't stop for long, we need to keep going," the Professor yelled. "The best crystals are at the heart of the cave system!"

Max swallowed. They'd barely made it this far into the caverns alive. "Rivet, perform a 3-D scan of the area."

Rivet wagged his stubby tail as his head rotated in a neat circle. "Ready, Max." His eyes lit up as he projected a map of the caverns.

Max counted over a dozen glowing tunnels. Some looked so tight that the aquafly would get wedged or torn to pieces. He traced their route. It dipped and twisted like the largest waterslides in Aquora, but it would take them all the way to the central cavern.

"Lia, Spike, hold on tight," Max said. "We'll have to ride the undertow all the way!"

Max blasted the thrusters in reverse and the craft shot from the crevice. He was thrown forward as the current snatched the sub again. He glanced through the watershield, glad to see that Lia and Spike had managed to cling on to the roof of the aquafly.

Max fought to keep the aquafly level, diverting as much power to the stabilising motors as he could. The craft groaned and creaked as the current pummelled it, then slammed it around another corner and another, before finally spitting them out into a great cavern. The roar of the water vanished, leaving only the distant howls of the caves.

The sub spun to a halt and bobbed in the water. Max tried to calm his churning stomach and glanced out of the viewing screen. He gasped. The cavern was huge! The entire Aquoran defence force could have fitted inside, twice over. Crystal formations sprouted from every surface of the cave. They glowed with an intense green light.

Max turned to the Professor. "What now?"

The Profession consulted his wrist computer before scanning the dead mindbug in the jar. "Considering you built him, your dogbot has been surprisingly handy." He shared the screen with Max. "If I reprogramme him to emit this frequency, then the crystal I need should resonate back. Then all we need to do is to fit it into the raygun at my secret lab, and use that to stop the mindbugs."

Max studied the figure on the Professor's tiny screen. It was an easy adjustment to make, but he didn't want the Professor messing around with Rivet's programming. "Leave that to me," he said. "I know how he works."

The dogbot froze as Max opened the panel behind his head. It didn't take long to adjust his sonar into a frequency resonator. Max checked the wiring that he had altered earlier and redirected the extra power away from his jaws and back into the propellers where it belonged. He closed the panel with a gentle click. "Time to go for a swim, Rivet."

Rivet's ears pricked up. "Yes, Max!"

Water filled the compartment before Max slid back the exit hatch and swam out into the ocean with Rivet. The humming of the crystals was loud, but not unbearable. The sound was clearly dampened in this central cavern. The Professor, still inside the sub, cleared his throat. "Do be careful," he said. "The whole cave is structurally unsound and could collapse at any moment. I wouldn't want to be buried alive here."

Max stared at the Professor, whose face was lit up green. *Why didn't you mention that before?* He'd have to work closer to the cavern walls and use a lower intensity on the frequency resonator. "You and Lia had better stay here, in case we need to get away fast."

"Of course, Max," said Lia, swimming nearby on Spike. "You do what you have to."

There was something funny about the way Lia was behaving, Max thought, but perhaps it was just nerves. He grabbed hold of Rivet's collar. "Up, Rivet!"

"Yes, Max!" Rivet's propellers whirled into action, lifting Max to the jagged ceiling of the vast cavern. Bright green crystals grew in impressive formations across the rock.

The dogbot sniffed and let his tongue hang out. He yawned with a high-frequency whine. Max pressed his hands to his ears before the comms headset tuned out the piercing noise.

Max pointed out a promising cluster of crystals, but as they swept past the noise had no effect on them. *I hope the Professor calculated the right frequency*, Max thought.

"Max!" Rivet barked, suddenly changing direction. He swam towards a very smooth, shiny crystal off to one side. Max didn't think it looked promising, but as the dogbot pulled him closer, he heard a high-pitched note coming out of it. It sounded like a tuning fork.

"Professor," Max called over the communicator. "I've found one!"

"You'll need to dig it out of the surrounding rock," the Professor replied. "Be careful as I need it in one piece. And, whatever you do, don't bring the ceiling down."

Max reached for a laser scalpel from the dogbot's storage unit and swam closer.

The crystal was about the length of his arm. Taking care, Max sliced rocks away from the base of it until it slid free. He examined it with a torch. Its surface was smooth and perfect. Now they had the first part of their weapon to defeat Siborg! He grinned, hope flooding his chest. His parents would be free in no time.

The sound of a blaster pistol charging up

behind him tightened all the muscles in his body. His face fell. It had just been a matter of time before the Professor would betray them. He slid out his hyperblade before closing the storage compartment over the crystal.

"Not so fast, Max!"

It wasn't the Professor's voice. Max turned around slowly and gasped. Lia was sitting on Spike's back, a blaster pistol trained on Max.

CHAPTER SEVEN

SIBORG STRIKES BACK

"What are you doing?" Max gasped.

Without lowering the blaster pistol, Lia swept her long silver hair away from her neck.

A mindbug nestled between her collarbone and her gills.

Max felt a chill of horror creep down his spine. "It can't be…"

The insect-like metal device was clamped onto Lia's neck. Its body pulsed with tiny red lights.

"Aren't I clever?" Lia said, robotically, and Max knew it was Siborg speaking. "My mindbugs can control the Merryn now."

Max shivered even under the thermolayers of his deepsuit.

"Lia not right, Max," Rivet barked.

"I know." Max gripped the hyperblade tighter, wondering if he could disarm her. "How did you get the pistol?" he asked her.

"Your father. He delivered it and planted the mindbug while we were on the bridge of the sub, and you were struggling with my worthless father," she replied. "Now hand over the crystal. Nothing can stand in the way of the conquest of Aquora!"

Max hesitated, his gaze fixed on Lia's webbed fingers around the blaster pistol. Without the crystal, the Professor's mindbug raygun wouldn't work. Max couldn't just hand it over, but he needed time while he figured out how to escape. "But why Lia and not me?"

"A technical issue. Infecting those with the Merryn Touch has proved slightly harder than expected," Siborg sneered through Lia's mouth. "Now, the crystal!"

Lia jerked the weapon towards him. Max glanced past her towards the aquafly. He clicked the comms button on the sleeve of his deepsuit. He just hoped the Professor would come to his aid. "I'll never give you the crystal, Siborg," he said loudly, so the Professor would hear. "I won't let you keep my parents or my friends as slaves!"

Lia yawned. "I see we will have to do this the hard way, then."

Over the eerie howl of the caves, a grinding noise echoed down from the far end of the cavern. Small crystals and sand shook from the ceiling and floated past. Then on the other side of the cavern, part of the wall collapsed as the torpedo-shaped head of Tengal burst out in a flood of churning mud and stones.

The Robobeast was like something out of a nightmare. Its grey eyes fixed on Max as it slithered forward, shaking more debris from the plated metal sections of its long, powerful body. The cavern shuddered ominously.

"Tengal tracked us, using my mindbug," Lia said. "This is your last chance to do this the civilised way."

Max swallowed. He and Rivet were totally at Siborg's mercy. And as he looked down, he saw the Professor steering the aquafly away from Tengal. *Is he leaving us?*

Their only hope was to get to the aquafly, fast. Max noticed a large emerald crystal above Lia that was still shaking from the entrance of the Robobeast. *It must be really loose*, Max thought. If he could just dislodge it…

"Up, Rivet!" Max yelled.

The dogbot's propellers whirled into action. Max was yanked towards the roof of the cavern as Rivet zoomed upwards and Max grabbed hold of his back legs. A blaster bolt exploded off the rocks close by. As Max neared the shaking formation, he swung his hyperblade, snapping off the crystal with a loud crack.

He struck it again as it fell. The crystal shattered into hundreds of pieces, creating a cloud of sharp falling fragments between him and Lia. Rivet zoomed to the side, and Lia's blaster bolts exploded harmlessly in the raining rock pieces.

Max urged Rivet on. "Quick, to the aquafly."

Rivet twisted towards the sub, but Tengal was surging at them from across the cavern. Its whirring teeth were beginning to spin. *We've got no chance against that powerful suction.* "Professor!" Max shouted over on the comms. "Deploy the depth charges!"

Ten black canisters blasted from the aquafly and hurtled through the water towards the Robobeast. They hit the creature's metallic plates, but then bounced off.

"No!" Max yelled.

The canisters spiralled down and exploded against the cavern floor.

Boom!

Max grabbed Rivet tightly as the shockwave rippled across the cave, sending blade-like crystals dropping through the huge cavern. Rivet was thrown sideways, but Max kicked out, directing them back towards the aquafly. Max fought against the current from the frilled shark's mouth. It was getting stronger by the second, as the beast began to suck its victims in. It whipped its metal tail and lurched towards Max.

Max reached the aquafly at last and grabbed hold of the hatch. He tried to open it, but it wouldn't budge. He banged on the watershield. "Open the hatch."

The Professor looked out at him and shook his head. "I've calculated the risk. Our chances of survival are increased if we split up," he called over the communicator. "Well, mine are, at least. Good luck! And try not to lose the crystal!"

His uncle yanked on the steering column. Before Max could grab onto the wings, the engines roared and the aquafly tore away.

Max stared after the aquafly, stunned, as it darted into a small opening and disappeared. He couldn't believe that his uncle had just abandoned him like that.

"No one can trust the Professor," Lia said.

Max turned around.

His friend sat astride Spike, who was fidgeting, flicking his tail. But Lia held the swordfish firmly. She levelled the blaster at Max. Tengal hovered close by in the water behind her.

So much for the Professor's calculations! Max thought.

"If you give me the crystal I'll make it quick. I can't miss at this range," Lia continued. "Or I can command Tengal to take it from you. That won't be so quick."

The metallic frilled shark rippled forward expectantly. Water foamed around its mouth as its teeth whizzed faster. Max shuddered. He glanced from Lia to the Robobeast and back again. He and Rivet didn't stand a chance against either of them.

Spike's sword was dipped and his eyes looked sad. *He's known all along that something was wrong with Lia*, Max thought. *We still have one ally in this cave.*

Max wished he had Lia's Aqua Powers and could talk to the swordfish. Instead he shouted, hoping the swordfish understood what he meant. "Spike, Lia unwell. Lia dangerous. Help me."

Spike's eyes darted up. His head tilted to the side as though he was thinking about Max's words.

"Enough games, Max," Lia snapped. "Time to die." As she fired the blaster, Spike squirmed and the shot went wide. Lia cursed and slapped the swordfish hard. "Behave!"

Spike bucked, throwing Lia off his back and into the water. The surprise sent the blaster flying out of her hand. Max dived after the pistol, kicking hard. But before he could get

his fingertips around the handle, the pistol was sucked away into Tengal's mouth. As it hit the whirring electric teeth, the blaster was instantly ground to scrap metal.

Max twisted around to escape the current, but it was no good – the Robobeast was dragging him more and more forcefully into its open jaws.

CHAPTER EIGHT

BURIED

"Help, Max?" Rivet called over the comms
"Just get away!" Max managed to
pant. He didn't want Rivet to be eaten as well.
Besides, his dogbot carried the crystal they
needed to defeat Siborg. Max swam with all
the strength he could muster against Tengal's
suction, but the frilled shark matched his every
move. *If only I had thrusters like the aquafly, I
could blast myself free before the Robobeast had
time to stop me*, Max thought.

He glanced at Rivet paddling above him, his

ears pressed down with worry. *Wait – maybe I do have thrusters...* "Rivet," Max yelled. "Fire thrusters straight down!"

"Yes, Max." A blaze of fire erupted near the dogbot's propellers, powering Rivet through the Robobeast's current close to Max.

Max was almost out of energy, but he reached up, grabbing hold of the dogbot's collar. "Keep going, Riv!"

The force of Rivet's thrusters almost pulled Max's shoulder out of its socket, but the pain was worth it. His dogbot swept him out of the current, and under the Robobeast's belly.

The massive creature swung round nimbly. Max scanned around for somewhere to shelter from it, and spotted a gnarled crystal formation rising from the cavern floor. "Over there!" He pointed, then dived away from Rivet as they reached the rock. "Hide, Rivet."

As the dogbot shot away, Max felt ripples

brush against his neck. He turned around and saw Tengal's plated body snaking around. It jerked through the water, quickly latching onto him again with its powerful suction.

Max wedged his hands into the crystal formation, trying to stay put. Chunks of crystal and rock snapped off from the cavern floor around him. He ducked the deadly pieces that shot past him into the Robobeast's whining grinders, but he held on tightly. *Crack!* One of the crystals under his hand broke apart and he snatched hold of another one.

Max turned to see pulverised rock streaming out from the shark's robotic gills, like green sand. *If only it would swallow enough rocks to clog up its throat,* he thought. He noticed stones falling from the cave roof, and looked up to see some of the giant stalactites vibrating, as if they might crash down at any moment.

Suddenly, Max was thrown forward as the

current stopped. Then he felt a rush of water as the Robobeast dived towards him.

It's going to try to snap me up the old-fashioned way! he realised.

The break in the suction gave Max the chance he needed. "Rivet, here, quick!"

"Yes, Max." The dogbot surged forward, and Max grabbed his collar again. His stomach lurched as the dogbot lifted him away. He felt a wave of force as Tengal crashed into the crystal where Max had been a second before. Rock fragments exploded into the water.

"Rivet, to the top of the cavern!" Max said, and Rivet's propellers whizzed into action.

Max watched the Robobeast snake across the floor, changing direction as though dazed. It shook its head, then reared up and stared around. Max felt its cold eyes spot him, and Tengal came soaring straight upwards.

I'll give you something to chew on, he

thought, as he spotted the biggest of the crystal stalactites close by. "Up there, Rivet," Max yelled. "Hit it as hard as you can."

Rivet fired his forward thrusters, almost throwing Max from his back as he slammed into it, sending out a spray of rocks and dust.

Crack! A fissure spread out from the impact.

The crystal groaned and Max wedged in his hyperblade like a lever. With a twist, he sent a large chunk sinking fast toward Tengal.

The Robobeast tried to swim away, but it was too late. The crystal formation hit its body, driving it hard into the cavern floor.

More rocks fell as the crack on the ceiling spread. Through the deadly rain, Max could see Tengal's body squirming, but it was pinned to the floor and couldn't escape. The jagged rock and hard crystal battered it. As the dust settled, Max saw the Robobeast's crushed head. Its eyes flickered once, then went dead.

"Robot broken, Max!" barked Rivet.

But there was no time to celebrate. More cracks were opening up all around them, and tremors made every crystal in the cavern shudder dangerously. *The cavern is collapsing!*

Max peered through the falling crystal, unable to see any sign of Lia and Spike. Then he heard a high chirp of distress. *Spike!*

He stared into the rubble below and saw blood rising from a pile of debris. Swimming closer, he saw that Lia's pet swordfish was pinned down by a fallen rock. His sleek blue body had been cut by the sharp crystal fragments, but he was still alive. Spike chirped again, his big eyes staring up at Max.

"Rivet, help me," Max yelled as he dived.

Spike was struggling to break free but his twisting was just causing him further injury. Max stroked the swordfish's head gently to calm him down. "Hold still. I'll save you."

He gripped the crystal with both hands and strained to lift it. All around him, boulders crashed against the rocky floor. His arm and leg muscles burned as he hoisted the crystal higher. "Quick, Spike," he panted. Spike wriggled forward, dragged his tail free and swam to Rivet. He squeaked with appreciation.

"Max!" Rivet barked. "Lia!"

Max dropped the crystal and looked to where Rivet's snout was pointing. Lia was diving into a tunnel on the far side of the cave. Spike swam forward, but then hesitated. Rocks rained down across the whole cavern.

He'll never make it to her, Max thought. *And besides, she's still under Siborg's control.*

"Spike, this way, follow us," Max shouted, pointing to another entrance to a jagged passageway. He grabbed hold of his dogbot's collar. "Rivet, fast as you can!"

Max clung on as the dogbot shot down the twisting tunnel. From behind, he heard the roar of the cavern finally collapsing entirely.

A tidal wave of water surged through the tunnel and slammed into Max's back, ripping him away from Rivet. "No!"

The white water seethed and bubbled, beating Max with invisible punches. He tried to grab hold of Rivet, but the dogbot was tumbling away. Max lost sight of him and Spike in the ferocious water. He was tossed against the walls like a rag doll, unable to stop himself smacking into them. Pain exploded through his body, and everything went black.

CHAPTER NINE

LAST HOPE

"Wake up, Max," Rivet barked, nosing him with his snout. "Worried!"

"I am awake," Max groaned. "It's okay, boy. I must have just blacked out."

The ocean was murky but he could see that he lay on the barren sand just outside the Howling Caves. He must have been thrown out through the tunnels by the tidal wave.

The huge outcrop of green rock had collapsed. Fine green sand swirled around, leaking from the remains like blood. The ocean was eerily quiet, apart from a series of low chirps coming from Spike.

Rivet's head suddenly raised up and the water churned as he rushed past Max's shoulder. Max looked back and saw the dogbot sniffing at a shining object nestled on a shard of rock on the ocean floor. *Lia's spear.*

"Where Lia?" Rivet barked. Max's chest tightened as he swam over to the Merryn weapon. She had escaped, hadn't she?

He glanced at Spike, floating beside him. The swordfish leaned to one side, flapping a single fin in distress. *He would have died if I'd let him try to swim across the cavern after her.*

Max could hardly believe it was happening. Lia was his best friend, and the thought of carrying on a Sea Quest without her made it hard for him to swallow. They were a team. *Where are you, Lia? Please be okay…*

Spike rubbed against Max's leg, and he

tried to comfort the swordfish as Lia would.

"It's okay," Max murmured. "She's too valuable to Siborg for him to let her get hurt."

Spike shook his sword from side to side. *I wouldn't believe it either*, Max thought, but he had to say something to cheer Spike up. "Rivet and I will look after you until we find her," he added. Spike's sword lifted slightly. It wasn't much, but it was a start.

Rivet's ears pricked up and he barked. "Something coming, Max!"

The rumble of an engine was approaching. Rivet huddled close to Spike to protect him, but Max already recognised the sound of the aquafly. One of its cylinders had been misfiring since their encounter with Tengal.

Max shook with anger as he remembered how the Professor had left him to face the frilled shark alone. If his uncle had rescued him and Rivet then the Howling Caves wouldn't have collapsed in the fight and Lia might have made it out. Max gritted his teeth. *I won't forgive you for this one.*

The aquafly wobbled as it slowed and dipped towards him. Dents and dust covered the once sleek, shiny body. Max noticed the paint had been scraped from the wings and the panels torn along the side. The craft hovered as the Professor opened the hatch.

"What are you waiting for?" he demanded. "We haven't got all day. Climb aboard."

Anger surged through Max as he clambered through the airlock, still holding Lia's spear. He stowed the weapon in the sub then climbed into the seat next to his uncle. "Lia might be dead because of you!" he yelled.

The Professor raised his eyebrows. "I'm afraid not," he replied curtly. "Look at this." He flicked on the small vid-screen on the aquafly's console. An image showed the rocky seabed, and Lia swimming away as bubbles exploded from a fissure.

Max felt a rush of relief, even thought she'd tried to kill him not long before.

"She made a break for it when the caves collapsed," said the Professor.

"Why didn't you stop her?" said Max.

The Professor rolled his eyes. "Because, dear nephew, I was looking for you! Count yourself lucky I came to see if you survived."

Max crossed his arms. He knew his uncle didn't care about anyone but himself.

"You and your dogbot have been surprisingly useful so far," the Professor went on. "Besides, you now have the only crystal we can use to defeat Siborg."

"First we're going to find Lia," Max said.

"Out of the question. Our priority is to reach my secret lab where we will be safe."

"But we could be her only hope," said Max.

"Lia will be on her way to Siborg already," the Professor said. "We need to concentrate on saving Aquora. Not to mention Sumara. After all, if my son was able to infect your fishy friend with a mindbug, then all of the Merryn are under threat."

Max hated to admit it, but the Professor

was right. If she were her normal self, Lia would have wanted them to stop Siborg.

"Besides, knowing my son, he'll find a way to follow us to my lab," the Professor added. "There isn't a second to waste."

Everything the Professor said made sense. Getting the raygun working was the most important part of their Quest now. Once they had the weapon and could disrupt Siborg's mind control, Max would search for Lia and free her from his evil cousin. He wouldn't rest until she was back by his side.

"Now, where is the crystal?" the Professor asked. "I need to start running some tests."

Max opened Rivet's storage hatch. The crystal sparkled as he removed it. Then he slipped reluctantly into the entrance of the aquafly, water draining behind him. "Here."

The Professor snatched the crystal from Max's hands and peered carefully at its

surface. He turned it over and over, whistling under his breath. "Excellent work," he muttered. "Now let's get to the lab, if this contraption of yours doesn't kill us en route."

"There's nothing wrong with my aquafly," Max replied. "It's got us this far, hasn't it?"

"Luck rather than design," said his uncle.

Max ignored the Professor as he checked the control systems. As long as the secret lab wasn't any further than his uncle claimed, the aquafly would get them there without major problems. "Which way?" Max asked.

"Keep heading west." His uncle pointed without looking up from his wrist computer.

Max activated the nav-screen and twisted the throttle. The aquafly surged forward, with Rivet and Spike following close behind.

As Max steered into the green gloom of the ocean, he glanced back at what was left of the Howling Caves. The thought of Lia in the grasp of Siborg made his stomach turn, but there were other lives at stake now. Not just those of all Aquorans, but those of the Sumarans too. It was up to Max to save them all, with only his crazy, evil uncle to help.

I've never failed a Sea Quest before, thought Max. He gripped the aquafly's controls and powered the vessel onwards through the ocean. *And I'm not going to start now.*

Don't miss Max's next Sea Quest adventure,
when he faces

KULL
THE CAVE CRAWLER

COLLECT ALL THE BOOKS IN SEA QUEST SERIES 6:

MASTER OF AQUORA

978 1 40833 480 5

978 1 40833 481 2

978 1 40833 483 6

978 1 40833 485 0

OUT NOW!

Look out for all the books in
Sea Quest Series 7:

THE LOST STARSHIP

VELOTH THE VAMPIRE SQUID
GLENDOR THE STEALTHY SHADOW
MIRROC THE GOBLIN SHARK
BLISTRA THE SEA DRAGON

OUT IN MARCH 2016!

Don't miss the
BRAND NEW
Special Bumper Edition:
JANDOR
THE ARCTIC LIZARD

OUT IN NOVEMBER 2015

WIN AN EXCLUSIVE
GOODY BAG

In every Sea Quest book the Sea Quest logo is
hidden in one of the pictures. Find the logos in books
21-24, make a note of which pages they appear on and
go online to enter the competition at

www.seaquestbooks.co.uk

Each month we will put all of the correct entries into a draw
and select one winner to receive a special Sea Quest goody bag.

You can also send your entry on a postcard to:

Sea Quest Competition, Orchard Books,
Carmelite House, 50 Victoria Embankment,
London, EC4Y 0DZ

Don't forget to include your name and address!

GOOD LUCK

Closing Date: Dec 30th 2015

IF YOU LIKE SEA QUEST, YOU'LL LOVE BEAST QUEST!

Series 1: COLLECT THEM ALL!

An evil wizard has enchanted the magical beasts of Avantia. Only a true hero can free the beasts and save the land. Is Tom the hero Avantia has been waiting for?

FERNO
THE FIRE DRAGON

978 1 84616 483 5

SEPRON
THE SEA SERPENT

978 1 84616 482 8

ARCTA
THE MOUNTAIN GIANT

978 1 84616 484 2

TAGUS
THE HORSE-MAN

978 1 84616 486 6

NANOOK
THE SNOW MONSTER

978 1 84616 485 9

EPOS
THE FLAME BIRD

978 1 84616 487 3

DON'T MISS THE
BRAND NEW SERIES OF:

Series 15: VELMAL'S REVENGE

978 1 40833 487 4

978 1 40833 489 8

978 1 40833 491 1

978 1 40833 493 5

COMING SOON